I0533849

Desired
Passion
Sexy
Stories
Collection

VOLUME 6

10 EROTIC SHORT STORIES

STERLING KLEMM

Desired Passion/ Sterling Klemm. -- 1st ed.
Xplicit Press, an imprint of TLM Media LLC

ISBN-13: 978-1-62327-535-8
ISBN-10: 1-62327-535-0
eISBN: 978-1-62327-587-7

Printed in the United States of America

CONTENTS

1 DIGNITY AND PASSION

Bob Bruce, born in 1845, never knew who his parents were since he was brought up in a mission called Sisters of Mercy in the southern part of the District of Columbia. It was learned that a colored newborn was found on the grassy inlay at the entrance of the mission by a sister who was returning from her visit to the hospital in town. The mission itself was located in the outskirts of the city, and they received rare visits from socially obligated patrons once or twice a month. The mission was run purely on charity, and in return the sisters conducted prayer meetings and supplemented help in the local hospital.

Bob was brought up in an environment where he quickly learned to use his strength in serving society. He would run errands for the older sisters, help in the kitchen, and sell bakery products made by the sisters during the bi-weekly market in town. The sisters took turns in teaching him to read and write, and this was a true blessing in disguise, which he learned later during his life. Bob earned the name "Giant" due to his height and brawny build. He could lift the heaviest of sacks with ease and carry them great distances.

No one knew why Bob always chose to wear trousers which had three pleats, quite an odd fashion. When the war broke out, the sisters discouraged Bob to enlist and fight alongside the Union soldiers. Finally, they gave in to his request and Bob joined the army. Bob, a fast learner, soon caught the attention of his senior commanders. Despite his limited knowledge of warfare, this 25-year-old African-American came to be known as a good strategist.

Unfortunately, once during a 4-hour gun battle with the Confederate soldiers, Bob was hit by a volley of bullets in his lower stomach. It was only due to immediate medical help that his life was saved. He was later informed that some portion of his abdomen had been damaged permanently. This meant that although he could indulge in sexual activity, he would not be able to become a father. Bob was given an honorable discharge and was sent to New York for recuperation.

During his six months of rehabilitation, he would receive a hamper of fruits once a week, distributed by a widow named Ms. Maureen Hampstead. Maureen had been widowed for just a year after she married a rich land owner named Tim Hampstead. Tim had enlisted to fight the Confederates and was killed in one of the battles. Maureen had mourned his death, but after a while stepped out to serve the injured soldiers at the hospital.

Once, while she was on her daily rounds, she chanced upon Bob, who had just woken up and was struggling to get up from his bed. She rushed to his side, helped him sit up, and then held the basin for him to gargle after he had brushed his teeth. She conversed with him for a while and learned about his background. Impressed by his humility, she promised to meet him every other day whenever she could get a chance.

Once, while helping him get up, her hand brushed against his manhood which had been tucked in tightly under his gown. The hardness and the size had startled her, and she had looked at the region in disbelief. She heaved breathlessly as Bob looked away in shame. Recovering from her initial shock, she had had merely patted his arm and called for an attendant to help Bob, as if nothing had happened, and then quickly strode away. On her way home, she was surprised by the dampness within her skirt and the heat spreading over her face. She tried to rid the thoughts from her mind by twisting her handkerchief, but to no avail. The hot flush returned together with reminisces of what her hand had touched. It disturbed her but also gave her some relief to know that there was hope for her.

Her early widowhood had left her bereft of any sexual release, and since she belonged to one of the respected families in town, she had abstained from any contact with coveting males who would approach her. Three days after this incident, she met Bob in the morning and offered him a job—to work as a butler in her house. Bob thought about it for a moment and then accepted the offer. The war had come to an end and a colored employee had come to be accepted.

Finally, after having completely recovered from his injury, Bob accompanied Maureen to her house which was located in the periphery of the town. It was part of a large estate, and it had sugarcane plantations as well as a huge cow shed. Maureen had been running the business on her own after the death of her husband. She lived in the house with six lady servants. Over fifty men had been in her employ, and they worked hard under her direct supervision. Maureen had decided to leave Bob in charge of this activity in addition to some of his personal chores as her butler. She had thought that in this way, he could justify his presence in the household as well.

On arriving home, she called for Betty, her personal maid, to show Bob his quarters, which was a cozy one-room cottage behind the main house. Betty was of mixed parentage. She was born out of wedlock to a black woman and a white trader. She had a wheat-ish complexion and a well-endowed body. On her mistress's instructions, she had done her best in cleaning the place, and it looked quite decent. Bob thanked her and entered his new living space. He couldn't help but notice Betty's large breasts as they struggled to keep hidden in her coarse maid's dress. Betty knew the effect she had on him and lingered closer to him until she could hear him breathing and her mouth fell open. If it wasn't for the shrill voice of her mistress, she would have risked a touch.

She hurried outside and responded to

Maureen's call. Upon Betty's entering the room, Maureen asked her to come to her side as she had some papers to be clipped and kept in the cupboard. She noticed that Betty's cheeks looked flushed despite the dark color of her skin. Just as she handed over the papers, she held Betty's hand and looked at her face sternly.

Betty mumbled something about the sun being too harsh on her skin and quickly looked away. The weather had worsened over the last few days, and the heat was at its tormenting best. Maureen, deciding to overlook the instance, asked her to take a tray of lunch over to Bob and told her to ask him to come over after he was done with it. Betty hurried out of the room and hid her joy at the prospect of getting to face the "huge man" yet again that afternoon.

Meanwhile, Bob had taken off his clothes and, now only in his underpants, stepped out to have a shower in the wooden closet just outside his home. Once inside, he stripped naked and sank into the wooden tub filled with water. A bar of soap and a cloth scrubber lay on a stool nearby. As he sank his body inside the tub, the head of his big cock bobbed out. He smiled and fondled it for some time. Then, he heard his name being called out twice. It was Betty. She must have come with some errand from Mrs. Hampstead.

"In here!" He shouted back. "I am taking a bath," he continued. "What is it that you want?"

"It's your lunch and I am going to keep it on your table," Betty replied. Lunch! Thought Bob as he was hungry. His appetite had gone up ever since he was in the hospital. He thanked Betty and continued to wash himself, straying now and then onto his cock. It was a bit bigger than the average size. The circumference was just right, but the length was more than he could manage. He had tried to shield his thoughts of his cock during his days at the Mission, but once when he had chanced upon the naked figure of Sister Trudy while she was bathing, he had felt an urge to masturbate but he did otherwise since the Mother Superior had warned him of the consequences.

That night he could hardly sleep as he lay in his bed, recalling the sight of those well-shaped breasts and her sleek and slender legs which tapered at her waist around the bushy hair. The thought of the pink skin under the hair was too much to bear. Now he was without any barriers, mental or otherwise, and he also knew that he would not bring risk to any woman he slept with because of his condition.

Outside the door of the closet, Betty chose to stay back after laying the tray of food inside and peek through the cracks between the planks. The shaded area was shielding her from being seen from the inside, and when she saw Bob's erect manhood, she stifled a scream.

It had been more than two years since she had been with a man and had spent horrendous moments alone in her bed at nights. She knew that there would be no one around at this time of the afternoon, and so she took the opportunity to look at the naked giant from her vantage point. Her hands had lifted her skirt over her thighs and exposed her hairy cunt. Pussy juice had already started to drip from her cunt as she dipped her finger tenderly into its velvety heat. Bob could see movement but he disregarded it. He stood up in the tub and scrubbed his body with the cloth. He knew that if Betty was watching, she would benefit from the view of his body.

Betty's anguish seemed clear on her face and she started to moan, not to be bothered if she was being heard. Her finger movements grew painfully frantic as she urged her lips to give in to her desire. Finally, she heaved loudly as a small jet of juice spurted out of her pussy.

She was lost to this world and did not even realize that Bob had stepped out of the closet with a towel wrapped around his middle. He looked down at her, astonished at her shamelessness, and called out her name. That was when Betty stopped midway, adjusted her clothing, and stood up. She apologized to Bob and ran into the house. Bob smiled and shook his head as he headed inside his home, ready to devour the lunch that was kept waiting at the table.

Lunch was simple: boiled corn on the cob, a large slice of meat with brown sauce poured over it, mashed potatoes, greens, and a jar of lemon juice. Bob cleaned the food off the plate and washed it down with the refreshing lemon juice. He then went to bed naked for a snooze. He was woken up by a wild knocking on the door.

"Who is it?" He called out. Betty responded to say that her mistress wished to see him at the house. Bob quickly splashed some water on his face and put on his clothes, then strode out towards the house, wondering what was in store for him.

His large frame looked ominous to anyone who would want to challenge him. As he knocked on the large door, Betty opened it and she stood by to let him pass. Her eyes were lowered, ashamed from the earlier incident, but Bob did not give it much attention.

He greeted her warmly and walked inside the house, his hat in his hand. Betty led him into a large living room. She asked him to wait for her mistress to arrive.

Maureen came into the room gliding gracefully and greeted Bob, and then asked him if he had found everything to his liking. Bob almost felt burdened with gratitude as he told her that it was more than he could have asked for.

"I have brought you in here to take charge of the workers on the estate. You will ensure that all the hands are working well," Maureen said.

She had a book of accounts in front of her on the table, and she pretended to be looking over the books while her eyes were staring at the mound which had risen in Bob's pants. Her cleavage was increasingly visible to the extent that her nipples were trapped just below the thick border of her dress. Her heart had missed several beats as she imagined being ravaged by this giant male standing in front of her. Her undergarments had already been stained with droplets of thick pussy juice that had dribbled along her thighs. She fought hard to keep her voice from faltering and managed to look up for a brief moment just to catch Bob's eyes to see if they revealed any mocking look at her condition.

Apparently, Bob was more concerned about holding this lady's attention with his efficiency more than anything else. After briefing him about the processes, Maureen asked him to saddle up two horses so that she could take him on a round of the estate.

It was dark when they had returned, and Bob took the reins from Maureen's hand, wished her good night, and took the horses to the stables. The trip had been uneventful except for the way the workers stared, wide-eyed, at the huge figure who rode beside their mistress. Maureen addressed the group of workers, introducing Bob and his role in the estate's affairs.

After their return, Bob decided to take a stroll in the woods behind his cottage. As he was walking on the pathway, lit only by the bright moonlight, he heard some noise behind him. He stopped to look behind but could not see anyone. His experience in the army told him to suspect otherwise, so he hurried further.

He came across a patch which was covered by the trees, and it was a bit dark in there. He quickly came and stood behind a tree, waiting. Just then, he saw a figure of a woman who rushed by and stopped. Bob grabbed the figure and put with one hand over the mouth. Then, he peered at the face. It was. Her body was light, and Bob could easily carry her towards the tree he was hiding behind.

"Why were you following me?" He whispered in a gruff voice.

Betty did not say a word but got out of his now loose grip and kneeled in front of him. She took off his belt and unbuttoned his trousers. Without another word, Bob leaned against the tree just to see what she was up to. Betty's gasp of astonishment was loud in the quiet of the woods when she drew out Bob's cock. She felt the length with one hand while her other hand roamed around his testicles. She seemed fascinated as she kissed the head of the cock a number of times. Then she put her mouth over it and began to suck it.

Her head bobbed up and down as she worked on the engorged manhood. Intermittently, she would stop and lick the entire length of the cock, then suck the slack skin around the testicle. All this was a new experience for Bob, and although he was astonished by the effect it had on him, he pretended to be in charge and held her hair in a fist.

Encouraged, Betty tried to take the whole length of the cock deep inside her throat, struggling a bit, but she was finally triumphant. That's when Bob stopped her and stood her up. He kneeled down and took off her white cotton underthings then raised her skirt. He then turned her around, exposing her wheat-colored rump. She let out a whimper while Bob pulled down the top of her dress, exposing her ebony-colored, well-rounded breasts. He squeezed them like one would squeeze watermelons. He was enamored by their softness and wanted to do more than what he was doing.

His cock was now poised just near Betty's steaming pussy, and he nudged it a couple of times. Meanwhile, Betty spat on her hand and reached behind to rub the spit on Bob's cock. Bob was surprised at her thoughtfulness and drove his cock inside her wet cunt. He had just about managed to insert a little less than half, and he pulled it back. He pushed it in yet again and then began the motion. He had set his limits for inserting his cock as long as he did not hurt Betty. She held on to the tree for balance and matched her movements so that they were in rhythm with Bob's.

Betty moaned and her hysterics had started to surface. She had never ever experienced such a good fuck in her life. In her own words, as she would later share with her co-workers in the house, the fuck was delicious. Bob had his hands over Betty's breasts, and he was pumping her cunt in slow and easy strokes. Betty was enjoying her time with her legs spread wide and was moaning intermittently.

After a while, she began to shudder as she was approaching her orgasm. Her shaking intensified as it hit her and she nearly collapsed, but Bob held onto her and brought her up.

His cock still inside, he turned her head towards his face and kissed her lips. They held that pose for quite a while and Bob felt indebted towards Betty for giving him such a good fuck. They were so involved that they failed to notice that they were being watched by another person. It was Maureen, who had remembered she needed to tell Bob that the following day was payday. She had chanced to see Bob walking towards the woods from the far end of the house and followed his steps. Her first thoughts were to severely reprimand Bob and sack Betty from her duties. But then immediately, good sense prevailed as she stomped back to the house, angrily.

Meanwhile, the two satiated individuals basked in their newfound intimacies. Bob had withdrawn his cock and Betty was licking it clean of all its juices. She looked up at Bob from her kneeling position with a pleased look in her eyes, as if to say thank you. Bob took a peek at his watch, which he drew from inside his coat, and persuaded Betty to hurry up and move back to the house. Betty did as she was told, but as she was walking towards the house, she could not help to steal glances at the "giant" who had just impaled her with his cock. She felt fondness and a sense of belonging after a long time.

Bob adjusted his cock inside his pants with a bit of remorse. He felt that he had taken advantage of the woman. "I wasn't like this at all," he said to himself. At the convent, he had earned the respect and love from all the sisters there with his work, but never like this.

He was reminiscing when he realized that the mistress had asked him to remain present in the house by 8:30 p.m. He looked at the watch and saw that he had but a few minutes to spare. He washed his face yet again and locked the door behind him. He strode towards the house in his swaggering gait and waited outside the door, having knocked once. He was surprised to see Maureen open the door for him this time.

"Come in," she said in her soft, graceful voice.

Bob walked in and stood a bit away until she had closed the door. He looked around for Betty to appear, but failed to see her. In fact, unlike the last time when he could see someone or the other, now no one seemed to be around.

"Come, Mr. Bob. Let's have some dinner," said Maureen. "I am afraid I have sent all the servants away for the day as it is their weekly night off," she spoke spiritedly.

Bob noticed that her cleavage was deeper and her breasts seemed to look a bit different. She had some perfume on and he could smell it as he followed her to the dining room. The table was set for two, one at the head of the table and the other on the left. Embarrassed slightly at this, Bob shuffled towards the table.

Maureen seemed cool, unlike her mood earlier that evening. She had thought things over and come to terms at that very moment. Yes! Bob was an employee and she had the right over him more than anyone else. But at the same time, she was living in a liberal society and her motives may not go down too well. Thus, she had changed her approach and was prepared to become more cordial to her employee.

Maureen excused herself and went into the kitchen to fetch the first course of the meal. She returned with a vat-like dish that contained soup. She then asked Bob to sit on her left and served him the soup. During the meal, Maureen tried to pry into Bob's life, his past, and other details. Bob felt obliged and told her about his life in the Mission and how he learned to read and write under the tutelage of the kind sisters.

Her attention was mostly drawn at the

time when Bob told her about his injury and his inability to father any children. Maureen was emotional while listening to Bob, and she even brought her handkerchief to wipe out a few drops of tears from her eyes.

The next course was a portion of lamb and vegetables. Bob began to feel honored at being served such a scrumptious meal, and he almost wanted to kiss the lady's hands for being so kind and generous. Maureen had understood that she had won his confidence, so after the meal, when Bob got up to help carry the dishes into the kitchen, she did not stop him. Bob felt good and as he came into the kitchen carrying the other plates, Maureen pretended to be busy and that she failed to see his presence. She brought her hand to her breasts and held them lovingly.

Bob was too stunned and he felt too embarrassed to even clear his throat. Just then, Maureen turned around and unabashedly called him over. Bob approached with caution as she sat on the edge of a table. She had raised her skirt, and since she had not worn anything under it, her pussy was open to be seen. Her pubic hair had been trimmed neatly, and there seemed to be a fragrance emitting from that region. Bob kneeled before her and drew his mouth close to her pussy. It looked good and well taken care of, or so he thought. He let his tongue probe the velvety hole and felt elation. He had never done this before because he had never had any such opportunity. Even when he was in the army, he had chosen to stay back, while his fellow soldiers would step out to revel with the women who would approach them in exchange of cash or some rations.

He licked the length of the steamy cunt, slowly relishing it in every way. After all, he was not going to let this kind lady down, who, after all these years, had suffered alone after being widowed by the cruel war. Maureen was just plain speechless and she felt the pleasures of this rampant promiscuous behavior absolutely marvelous. She had held on to her sexual enjoyments only in her mind, even though numerous opportunities had presented themselves in the past. Her dignity in the social circles remained firm as stone, and she had gained tremendous respect in the bargain. Now with this man, she found hope at the end of the tunnel. Her breathlessness began to show, so Bob stopped for a moment and asked if she was alright.

All Maureen could muster was a smile and a nod, urging him to go on. Now Bob knew that he had to take charge of the situation, so he stopped and stripped off his clothes. He then turned his attention to his mistress and began to untie the laces of her dress in a very patient manner. Maureen was too surprised to speak, and she stood motionless while Bob continued to strip her. Once they were both naked, he held her close to his body and kissed her, moving his tongue inside her mouth. He tasted her mouth and found it sweet, while his mouth had the taste of the fresh mint he had taken to chew before he had come. The mint-chewing habit was formed during his years at the Mission as it was a regular practice among the sisters. It was meant to keep bad breath at bay.

After a short time, he had had this woman completely surrendered to his whim, and her near-limp body encouraged him to do as he liked. Bob picked Maureen up by placing his hands under her shoulders, and he lifted her just above his waist. He urged Maureen to spread her legs and grasp his waist with them; Maureen did just that and locked her feet just behind his tight buttocks. Bob slowly lowered her body so that his hard and erect cock would impale her dripping cunt. Just as he began doing it, Maureen let out a soft whimper and sexual arousal was beginning to rise. Her voice resembled a young girl who was being treated to her favorite candy. Bob felt his cock being covered by the hot insides of this stunning woman. Maureen's cunt lips enclosed his cock tightly, allowing just enough of it to enter at a time. She did feel a little pain, but it was gone after a while as Bob began to raise her higher and then lowered her again. He did this with ease and Maureen put her arms around his shoulders and held her elbows so that she could be closer to this wonderful man.

Bob shifted his hands to hold her buttocks and to grip them, one in each hand. He sporadically squeezed them, sending waves of pleasure up her spine, and she squealed in her impish voice. The first wave of an orgasm began to surface, and Maureen began to bite her lower lip and her breathing began to rush out. Her heart was pounding and her mind was in a tizzy when suddenly she let out a wild scream and nearly fell out of Bob's grasp. Her head was facing the ceiling while her eyes were tightly shut. She could hardly breathe, and in a flash, she slumped over Bob's shoulder.

She could hardly believe when she said "Thank you, Bob," in a faint whisper.

Bob had never realized that he could enjoy his sexuality to such an extent, and he pulled out of Maureen's dripping pussy. He then put his hands under her knees and carried her upstairs to her bed. Lying her down, he covered her and was about to walk away when he heard her calling out his name. He stopped and returned by her side.

"Let me tell you this now. I shall never ever wish to have any other man in my house." She spoke in a whisper. "I know I have already found one," she smiled as she said this.

Bob nodded and held her hand in his for a while, and then, he smiled at her before rising and walking out of the door of the room.

2 THE PASSION OF SUBMISSION 1: THE HUNGER

Katrina grew up as an only child. Her father ran a steady plumbing business and her mother worked as a part-time waitress at a nearby diner. Her father was strict in bringing her up while her mother was compassionate to her feelings and often chided her husband on his attitude.

Time went on and in just after she had celebrated her 18th birthday her mother's sister came for a visit, accompanied by Javier, her neighbor's son, who was 20 years old. Her aunt and her family lived in San Diego but Javier was doing an internship in an architect's firm in San Jose, California. She and Katrina's mother had been very close but they had not seen each other in years. Javier had accompanied "Aunt Renee" both because she was too old to travel alone and because he was eager to see the structures in the city of Phoenix as part of his class project for the final year. Javier was a pleasant boy and he quickly earned Katrina's respect. She would follow him everywhere and take keen interest in whatever he would be doing.

One afternoon, Kayla took her sister shopping and Javier was in the spare room reading a book. Katrina had just stepped out of the shower, drying her hair. She thought she was alone and walked through the hallway naked. Halfway to her room she passed the open door of the room Javier was staying in and she saw him sprawled on his bed, reading a book. He looked up and just stared at her before beckoning her to come closer.

Mesmerized by his boldness, she approached the bed and sat down. Javier raised his hand to touch her face, which made her smile. She felt good as he slowly ran his hand across one of the breasts. She closed her eyes to hide her shyness. Javier felt the smooth skin and sat up, bringing his face closer to hers and kissed her cheeks and then her lips. It was an awkward kiss but for that moment it added to the thrill. Katrina felt his other hand come over her second breast and her nipples perked up. Her heart started to beat faster and her breathing increased. She was enjoying this electric sensation and she felt an odd tightness between her legs. Something sticky was oozing from her vagina.

Javier brought his tongue to lick her nipples. She stiffened and opened her eyes slightly to take a peek at what was going on. Just then they heard a car pulling up in the drive. Katrina's mother and aunt were back. Quickly, Javier retracted his hands and motioned her to leave the room. Katrina ran to her bedroom and dressed hurriedly. She quietly stepped out and went to the living room just when the door opened. The two women seemed quite happy and were busy chatting and laughing.

"Come Katrina, see what we picked up for you," said her aunt.

From a bag she brought out a beautiful silk scarf. Katrina smiled, eyes glowing and that was when Javier entered the room. He looked hesitantly at Katrina, worried she would tell on him for what he had done to her. Katrina looked back at him and merely smiled. The look on her face said "Don't worry." Javier smiled at her and sat on the sofa with relief written all over his face.

It was her first time being touched, but

she was positive it would not be the last.

Katrina had grown a bit curious about herself. Like any other girl her age, she was into chatting on the net with faceless. She had also chanced upon some sites which gave out information on something called BDSM, a lifestyle in itself.

During her spare time she would be found in front of the monitor, sometimes even well past midnight. The more she read and saw details about it, the more she wanted of it. Reading profiles on BDSM sites brought moistness between her legs. She was keen to leave her parent's home and live on her own, maybe in a different city, maybe somewhere in California. Her uncle ran a home maintenance business in downtown Los Angeles. She could help him in his business. She decided to ask her uncle if she could have a job and live with his family until she could find a better situation and to her surprise and joy, he said yes.

She arrived at LAX and walked out, taking in her new environment. There seemed to be a lot of energy around and she smiled at the prospect of better days ahead. She had been told by her father that she would have to go to the parking lot of the airport to be picked up. She had just come out of the concourse when she heard her name being called out. She turned around to face a handsome man with a square face. His well- built body was dressed in jeans and a checked shirt.

"Hi, I'm Lincoln. Welcome to LA," he said extending his hand.

"Hi," said Katrina cautiously.

Lincoln's cologne wafted into her nostrils as he explained that he was her Uncle Antonio's business partner and since he was stuck in some work he had asked Lincoln to pick her up.

"My car had broke down when I was on my wy here so we'll have to take a cab. Follow me," he said and began to walk ahead, not bothering to help Katrina with her luggage.

That annoyed her a bit but she set it aside and quietly followed him quietly. Lincoln whistled for a cab to stop as one was passing them. The cabbie came around and he opened the door for Katrina. The cab zoomed off towards their destination.

"How do you like the place?" he inquired and moved closer to her.

"It's looking good," she answered suddenly conscious about his looming body close to her.

Lincoln continued to speak and moved his arm closer to his elbow almost brushing her breast. What he did next was a bit quirky. He planted his right hand just between her legs on the seat. Now his forearm was touching her crotch and it was sending sensations to her pussy. Katrina tried to hold it and pull it away and in doing so brought it closer to her breasts. The effect was electrifying as she nearly let out a soft moan, which was unheard by the driver but Lincoln did get to notice it. He had now firmly wedged his hand between her legs pushing it deeper and using his elbow to rub her nipples.

Lincoln whispered into her ear, "Just enjoy the ride and leave the rest to me. Is that clear kitten?"

Katrina nodded. She was doing exactly as she was being told and her sexuality seemed to have heightened in the process. She found that she liked being told to do things. She was curious now, eager to know what would come next. Katrina wanted these moments to stretch for hours. Uncle Antonio's establishment was still some distance away and there was still a little time.

"Are you enjoying yourself?" he asked.

"Yes," responded Katrina, meekly.

"You will get more of this soon enough once you are settled in. Would you like that?" he continued.

"Oh yes, I would like that," she said with a smile, surprised by her response.

Midway, Lincoln asked the cabbie to pull over at the curb near a car which was being attended to by a mechanic. "Look, the cab will take you to your uncle's place while I get this car fixed." he told Katrina and stepped out.

The cab dropped her outside a beautiful yet simple two story home, where her Uncle Antonio was waiting for her.

"Oh, mi querido," he exclaimed and spread open his arms.

Running into his arms Katrina felt a sense a relief and security. She kissed his cheeks as he kissed hers. He asked one of his workers pick up her bags and take them into the office.

"Katrina, your aunt has been rather unwell or she would have been here to greet you," he said apologetically.

"It's ok Uncle Antonio," she answered. He said that due to her ill health she had become very irritated and would curse loudly. He did not want her to face his wife and thus had made arrangements for Katrina to stay above the office. As he explained, he took her upstairs and Katrina was happy with what she saw. It was a three room apartment with the living room facing the road; then at the back was the kitchen and further on was the bedroom with an attached bathroom.

"Wow, Uncle Antonio, thank you so much. This is perfect!" she exclaimed.

While her uncle left her to unpack and get ready, Katrina went into the bathroom for a shower. Once in the confines of the locked room, she stripped and looked at herself at the mirror. She smiled at herself, happy at what she was getting into. She was going to have fun in whatever form it came to her. Her hand slipped to her groin and she ran her fingers up and down her pussy lips as a moan slipped out of her lips. She heard her uncle call out her name, so she had a quick shower. Dressed now in fresh clothes, she came down the stairs. Her uncle introduced her to the other staff members. They all greeted each other and then her uncle proceeded to explain to her about his business and her duties. "I shall be paying you three hundred dollars per week," he said. Katrina happier than back home when she was earning a measly paycheck and tips.

Since Katrina was familiar with computers, Antonio gave her a laptop which had all the billing details. She was going through the details when a car pulled in and Lincoln came into the office. He waved at her and went into Antonio's office. After a while he left and went out again to his car. He brought a bag and returned handing over the bag to Katrina. "This is for you, for tonight," he whispered so others would not hear him. She did not understand, but nodded her head and went back to work. By evening, every one of his staff members had returned and handed over their bills and Katrina had almost completed her entering her figures. Uncle Antonio came and hugged her before leaving. By six o'clock she was all alone. Her uncle had ordered pizza which would be delivered by seven. It was paid for so there was nothing to worry about. Katrina shut out the lights save a lone bulb then went upstairs to see what was in the bag.

What she saw took her breath away. Inside was a short black dress which just about covered her thighs. There was also a note with a simple "No panties under this dress," written on it. There was also a mauve colored invitation card for a party. It had a set of instructions on the dress code as well as three phone numbers. What caught her eye was matter regarding the dress code. Women were advised to wear corsets, latex, lingerie and other fetish wear. Her heart beat a little faster as she wondered if her dreams of experiencing BDSM were about to come true.

Katrina was excited at the prospect, so she dressed and once ready she awaited

Lincoln's arrival. When he did show up Lincoln was dressed in black leather. Once in the car he told her about the party. He slid his hands up and down her naked thighs, sometimes touching her wet cunt. He spoke at length about the BDSM lifestyle. She was able to understand some of it, but it was still not very clear. Finally he told her to be herself and that she would be okay.

On reaching the venue they were warmly greeted by a group of people. Two of the women were topless and their pants had openings in the crotch section exposing their clean shaven cunts. Katrina was embarrassed as well as excited and she held on tightly to Lincoln's arm. Men and women were mostly dressed in skimpy clothes. There were a few women serving liquor and wearing nothing more than black thongs. Most of them were extremely attractive.

Lincoln's hands held her naked buttocks. He stroked her cheeks, raising her heart rate once again. Then he brought out a leather leash from his pocket. He held it around her neck and quickly buckled it firmly leaving some space in between. Then without any warning he pulled up her dress over her head leaving her completely naked.

Katrina was confused and scared. What was to become of her now? Would she be also paraded naked around like the others? Would all the guests also touch her body inappropriately? She steeled her nerves and shut her eyes against Lincoln's chest. He was holding her and she realized that she need not have any fears. She trusted him. Lincoln meanwhile turned himself to face the crowds and as she stole a peek she saw that all the women and a few of the men too had stripped off all their clothes and were hugging their partners. One by one they approached her and wished her a warm welcome. They smiled kindly and that was when Katrina's fears vanished. A few of the women kissed her cheeks and she responded evenly.

"This, ladies and gentlemen, is Katrina," announced Lincoln grandly.

Katrina felt a surge of anticipation and excitement within her. Gone were her fears and insecurities. She felt almost owned. But the feeling was nice and gave her goose bumps as well as some moistness between her legs. The night went by with couples indulging in rough sex quite openly. Time and again Katrina's hand slipped between her legs only to be slapped away by her Lincoln. She immediately understood the implication. From now on, she could not do as she pleased; she would do as she was permitted. What made her most happy was the fact that she felt like one of

Lincoln's possessions, like his car. She saw a bit of her father in Lincoln and that enhanced her feeling of lust.

The next day was a Saturday and she knew that office would be closed. She lazed a bit in bed mulling over what she had experienced the night before. She had a mild headache as she forced herself out of bed.

Her cell beeped and she picked it up. "See you tonight. Tonight will be your turn," the message read and she immediately thought of the women being spanked and tied down and the way they had looked as deliciously helpless as they begged to be fucked by the person who had been topping them.

Katrina was extremely nervous, and fretted about it for hours. She tried to relax by taking a long shower, but to her surprise she found herself becoming incredibly aroused. The very thought of being naked and taking Lincoln's cock inside her mouth and later in her pussy had sent some pleasurable shivers over her body. She braced herself to keep from falling with a massive orgasm that had made her breathless. Afterwards, shaved, painted, curled and sprayed with a perfume she had found in the bag he had given her she was ready to dress as she was told; no bra, no panties, just black thigh high stockings, a button-down blouse, tight, short black skirt, and black stiletto pumps. She took out her blouse and got into her skirt.

She heard her door open just as she was putting finishing touches to her face. It was Lincoln. Her heart skipped a beat as his tall daunting frame stood at the door of her bedroom. As she turned to face him smiling nervously he put his hands on her waist and then he kissed her. Katrina let out a soft whimper as she felt his lips on her neck and she closed her eyes in lusty anticipation.

He told her to bend over the bedside and brace herself while flipping her skirt over her hips. He inserted his fingers inside her dripping cunt to check and chuckled with satisfaction. He brought his fingers to her mouth to lick and suck clean. Katrina sucked his fingers to taste her own moistness. Meanwhile, the head of his hard cock found its objective as he shoved it in with some effort. Katrina gasped with the sudden, intense and deep penetration. A moan of pleasure escaped her lips as he drew his cock roughly in and out of her pussy. Just as she was getting ready to peak she let out a shrill scream as he withdrew his cunt-slimed cock and shoved it in her tight little asshole. He silenced her with his hand over her mouth and plunged even deeper and in some time he heard her roar in release as his semen spurted into her crack.

"I guess you have been initiated," he laughed as he commanded her to get a hot towel to clean him up. When she brought the towel he told her to kneel before him to clean him.

Then he tied her hands behind her back, and forced her legs wider apart, her kneecaps scraping the carpet.

"Open your mouth," Lincoln ordered.

She did as she was told and he unzipped his leather pants once again to bring out his massive cock, the same one which had some time back ravaged her holes to no. She took it in her hand and stroked it lovingly. Then she ran her tongue up and down the length of his cock. She sucked his balls for a while giving him some pleasure as the cool air blew in from the sea.

"I want you so badly," Katrina whispered as she gave him her mouth. "I want you to fuck me, please."

Her passion rose out from her submission to a man who was twice her age and who reminded her of her father.

3 THE PASSION OF SUBMISSION 2: THE LIFESTYLE

Katrina had taken to her new lifestyle like a fish in water. She had started to like her newly acquired "status." From the day of her initiation, she was required to go through her training period which required for her to be patient and obedient. It was only that she lacked patience. She went about her business at work without any problems, except that she became more alert in the presence of her Master, Lincoln. But Lincoln on his part did well as if nothing had changed.

He greeted her as he would greet others. But, come the weekend, especially on Saturday afternoon, she would be at his place cleaning his house and doing his laundry, all this in the nude. She had already told her uncle that she would be spending her weekends at the house of one of her work mates. She had explained to her co-worker that she needed to cover for her as she was meeting her boyfriend from Arizona, but her uncle couldn't know. Her co-worker, Marlene, was only too happy to oblige since she was the boss's niece.

The first Saturday, she was nervous so she accepted help from her friend Alisha. Alisha, as she knew, was a seasoned slave; hence she was fully aware of the duties of a slave. She met Alisha early that morning at a park which had a food court attached to it. Over coffee, Alisha told her that Lincoln had handed her a note for her to read and understand. Katrina opened the note and it read like this:

My dear slave Katrina

I WISH you to go through this very carefully and then if in agreement, we shall take it forward.

This is a list of the basic rules I use. This is a starting point, and not a comprehensive list of all the rules I would expect a fully trained slave to be adhering to. sSlave/trainee should take care of her health. This includes:

- She will not smoke

- Eating correctly (no excess food, no starvation, and watch your nutrition intake)

- Regular exercise (something aerobic, at least 30 minutes every other day)
- NO DRUGS! At any cost (Unless prescribed by a doctor)
- Regular sleeping patterns

This is not limited to the above.

- The slave/trainee shall not pleasure herself, nor allow others to give her pleasure except by the permission of her Master/Trainer. This includes:
- Masturbation
- Kissing, petting, fondling
- Sex (oral, vaginal and anal)
- Cybersex
- Phone-sex

Again the list of examples is not comprehensive. Further slave/trainee shall be prepared to do any of the above at her master/trainer's whim.

The slave/trainee shall not make modifications to her appearance except by permission of her Master/Trainer. This includes:

- Haircuts
- Piercings
- Tattoos
- Shaving of pubic hair
- Tanning/Tan-lines
- Cosmetic surgery

Again this is not a comprehensive list. Further slave/trainee shall make any changes requested of her by her Master/Trainer except as excluded in our contract.

The slave/trainee shall answer any question asked of her by her Master/Trainer completely, openly and honestly. The slave/trainee shall obey her Master/Trainer to the best of her ability and strive to please him at all times. If she is in doubt about exactly what is requested of her, or how to perform her duties she shall ask for clarification.

The slave/trainee shall keep a diary each day and make said diary available to her Master/Trainer.

As you can see, these are general rules and they do not cover the minutiae.

Your Master

On going through the note, Katrina realized that any reference made of her in the same would appear in lowercase, while the M in master was in the upper case. She looked up at Alisha in surprise and asked "What if I make a mistake? What happens then? Will he leave me?" Alisha smiled impishly and said "No, he will not leave you but you will be punished!" "What kind of punishment would that be?" Katrina asked. Again Alisha smiled, this time brightly. "Have you ever been spanked?" She said naughtily.

"What do you mean like on my bottom?"

asked Katrina. "No," she replied, embarrassed now. But a smile appeared on her face. After a while, Alisha dropped her at Lincoln's house. It was situated on a small hill in Pacific Palisades, an affluent neighborhood. This house was inherited by Lincoln from his father who had been a story writer attached to Universal Studios. As Alisha zoomed away, Katrina nervously walked to the driveway of the house and saw Lincoln wave out to her and beckon her over. Her heart was thumping already.

She was dressed in her favorite white shirt which was tied in the front and exposed her cleavage very neatly. (That had been his very first instruction to her). "Always keep your cleavage visible for My eyes only" he had said. Her jeans were low hipped exposing her cute navel. She had tied her hair up pulling it together in a nice ponytail. Her neck had the leather leash, which she wore in the car.

She stood outside the door, waiting for Lincoln to open it but instead heard his raspy voice coming from within. "Whatdaya waiting for? Christmas?" he roared. Nervously, Katrina pushed open the door and walked stealthily inside the house looking around, trying to familiarize herself with the interiors.

The house was gorgeous and it was very tastefully decorated with artifacts placed in the right places along with frames on the walls. Right ahead was a set of French windows which opened to a lawn with white fences at the far end. She walked further and beyond the fence, she saw could see part of the city below.

She was still staring at the view when Lincoln approached her from behind and held her breasts. He went straight to her neck and began kissing her relentlessly while his hands got busy unbuttoning her shirt and bra. He threw both on the floor and continued to massage her breasts. Katrina let out a wild moan and quietly brought both her hands behind and softly gripped her Master's cock through his pants.

It felt odd but she could feel it getting harder in her hand. She curled her hand gently around his balls but now she was eager to taste it in her mouth. She dare not make any move unless her Master told her to, so she just settled to relish his big hands on her breasts.

Lincoln loved what he was doing and also the fact that he had received a gift of the girl as his slave. He ordered her to remove his cock out of the pants. She unzipped his pants and surprised at not finding any other clothing, felt his hard cock in its full length. She was just about to draw it out his pants when she felt a sharp pain in her breast. Her Master had slapped her breast. "Bitch, whenever I ask you to do something, you have to respond with a 'yes, my Master,' " he growled.

The pain stung her but it also brought a tingling sensation to her now wet pussy. In fact she almost felt a trickle of moistness escape her cunt. "Yes, my Master," she whispered. She continued to massage his cock, now erect, and her excitement grew as she ran her hand up and down the length of it. She faintly recalled the time when she had licked it at the Pier on that night she was "collared." It felt so good that she began to get the urge of touching her pussy to take some relief, but dared not to.

Her experience was slowly beginning to advance in small steps and each step gave her more "freedom." Her passions were being ignited as never before. She could feel a dull ache on her breasts but she knew she would have to learn to bear it. It was not something she would do away with ease. Then almost on cue, Lincoln stopped and turned her around and asked her to remove his trousers. "Yes, my Master," she responded and did as she was told. Then moving back to a sofa he sat down and brought his lips to her breasts. Initially he flicked his tongue over her nipples which by now had now become painfully erect.

Katrina savored this pain with joyous pleasure. Her exploration had just commenced and she felt she was beginning to enjoy what she had been missing in her life. Lincoln closed his mouth around her nipple and began to suck on it as a hungry child would. Katrina could not bear the sensation as she nearly fell over.

"Oh my God!" She exclaimed without realizing that she was not supposed to. But this time, her Master chose to ignore it since he too was immersed in his lustful enthrallment. He took her whole breast in his mouth and ran is tongue over it. He had by that time whisked away her jeans and the black thong she had worn for the occasion. He held her tight buttocks in his large hands and gave them a good squeeze, increasing Katrina's pleasures to a higher level.

She whimpered lustily and curled her hands around his head encouraging him to do as he pleased. Lincoln brought his hands and ran it along her inner thighs going all the way up. His hands felt the creamy pussy juice and he felt her tremble with desire. He inserted three fingers and rolled them around the walls as she squealed in delight. Then he ran it up to her clitoris, giving it a good rub for a while.

This had her reaching her first orgasm. She shrieked in a piercing voice to which Lincoln brought his hand and gave her a resounding smack right on her buttocks. She was subdued instantly but she loved it. She loved the fact that she was being restrained of her expressions of feeling release. Lincoln realized that this girl was peaking well and stopped sucking her. He removed his mouth and had her kneel between his legs.

Now this was the moment Katrina was waiting for as she was in rapture even as she had taken him in her mouth for the first time but was disappointed when it was abruptly withdrawn. She took a moment to admire this piece of manhood and caressed it gently, lovingly making each stroke count as her soft hands did wonders to the erection. Then she ran her tongue along the whole length of the penis taking some time to tickle the testicles with her wetness.

Then she took the knobby head into her mouth running her teeth along the rim, and the tiny aperture on the head, just as Alisha had directed her to do. This brought a howl of pleasure from her Master and he moved his head from side to side, happy that he had made a good conquest. He held her hair firmly in his hand and began to direct her to blow his cock in and out of her mouth. Katrina did not need any more instructions as she took to suck the manhood with renewed vigor.

"I can never tire of this," she thought as her pleasures had started to mount. It was not long when Lincoln let out a cry which sounded like he was in anguish. His release came spurting out and he threw up his hands in an ultimate surrender to the moment as semen flew all over Katrina's face and hair. She managed to catch some of it in her mouth which she swallowed hungrily. She tried to lick some of it off her face.

"Katrina, my darling, you are my precious jewel and you have earned your servitude under Me," he explained happily. He raised her to her feet and had her sit on his lap curling her body into a ball so she could rest her head on his shoulder and her feet on one his thigh and her buttocks planted on the other. She could feel the pent up cock against the crack of her buttocks and she felt really secure.

"I shall not leave the confines of these arms for my whole life," she thought. In a while, he roused himself and asked Katrina to fetch a hot towel to wipe his now flaccid manhood. He also asked her to cleanse herself and pushed her gently to stand up and go. Katrina was a bit annoyed by this, but she hid her thoughts and walked into the bathroom. Her eyes turned wide as the bathroom itself was as big as her bedroom. It had a Jacuzzi and a shower cubicle with several shower spouts at various levels. She found the small towels neatly rolled in a small cane basket near the sink.

She opened the tap to let the hot water soak the towels. She then squeezed them dry and quickly walked to Lincoln, who was talking on his cell phone. She knelt in front of him and gently held the object of her desire. With slow tender motions she cleaned it with the warm towel reaching even the lower parts of his testicles, while her master ran his fingers through her hair, even as he spoke animatedly on his phone.

After having done her job, she waited in the same position waiting for his approval. She got up only after he nodded at her. Inside the bathroom now she put on the shower and drenched her entire body, waiting for the heat of the water to sensitize her skin. The shower cubicle comprised three sets of shower spouts. There was one set right above her head, the next was the one which could send a stream right across her face and chest, the one after that was aimed at the torso. The mechanism provided an option of a swirling shower, a straight jet and a sprayed shower in all of the spouts.

Turning around she allowed the jets of steaming water massage her back. Just as she was trying the different knobs to experience the various sensations as she aahed excitedly, she failed to hear Lincoln enter the bathroom.

He stepped close to the shower cubicle and slid it open. Katrina sensed a presence but waited as hands enclosed her bountiful breasts. She squealed and pretended to struggle meekly as Lincoln held her closer to his body. His engorged cock slapped at her buttocks as if warning her. He kissed her shoulders through the jets of water pouring over them.

The taste was somewhat sweet while Katrina raised both her hands in surrender. Lincoln held his cock and moved it closer to the crack of her ass and rubbed his cock against it, drawing cooing sounds from her. His other hand was busy on her breasts, clasping both in one hand and squeezing them hard, he enjoyed the sensation on his hands. He pinched the nipples hard enough for her to cry out loud. His fingers gripped the nipples even tighter that it now brought tears to her eyes.

He turned her around now releasing her breasts and kissed the nipples gently. He held her under the thigh and raised it higher so she could gain a foothold on the ledge at the bottom of the cubicle. This way, her cunt lips opened wide, allowing a good passage for Lincoln's now erect cock. He allowed himself to play with her lips before thrusting his rock hard member deep inside the warm honeypot.

His member was now enclosed completely, he spoke in her ears. "You will now take some lessons in restraint," he said. "I shall be fucking you for a long period, but you will hold your orgasm at bay," he said. Katrina looked at him in dismay as she knew that she could never control her orgasm. Lincoln's cock was already creating the passage for the magical moment, but she clasped her lips together hoping that this could stem the fallout. Instead, it enhanced her sensation. Within no time she gave out a shrill cry and came. Lincoln continued to thrust his cock without remorse into Katrina's cunt. He had felt her cunt constrict around his cock and knew that she orgasmed.

He had wanted that as now he could demonstrate to her the true meaning of what obedience meant in their relationship. After he achieved his release, he pulled out of her in a manner as if she was nothing. This left Katrina stunned. She whimpered as she felt her second orgasm just about to break and yet she had to stop it. She tried her best and almost collapsed in the tub, but put out a he hand to break her fall. Lincoln, in the meanwhile, had wiped himself dry and walked out of the bathroom calling her to follow him out.

Once out his voice trailed out from a different room. It was in the basement, and it had a sinister feel about it. The walls were covered with black leather and some parts looked as if they had been cushioned. In the middle was a wooden horse like structure with leather straps. She could also see that in the far side of the room, handcuffs had been fixed on the walls. Just as she was about to enter the room, Lincoln asked her to stop in her tracks.

"Kneel and enter the room in all your fours," he said. Katrina did as she was told and crawled into the room as Lincoln walked around her slowly examining her body from all angles. He enjoyed doing it to his slaves. His cock leapt about when he saw the pussies of the women from behind just as he was getting to see Katrina's moist cunt.

Her well rounded breasts dangled and moved like pendulums, enticing his craving to touch and hurt them even more. It was the thrill that made him what he was: the most admired Dom in the community. As Katrina came in the middle of the room, Lincoln told her to stop. He approached her from behind and blindfolded her with a black piece of cloth. Then he pushed her to the floor and hog-tied her. Her arms were hurting as they felt pulled hard towards her feet. She wanted to scream out but just then Lincoln gagged her mouth with a piece of rubber ball attached to leather straps which were quickly bound behind her neck.

Now the show was even more enticing for Lincoln as he chuckled. "You will remain in this position for half an hour, since you disregarded my instructions of not to have an orgasm," he said. "Orgasm denial is part of your training and it has to adhere to very strictly," he continued. She nodded in a. Lincoln walked away from the room upstairs and for some time all was silent in the room. After a few minutes "Sting" started to belt out his old track:

"Every breath you take,
Every move you make,
Every smile you fake,
Every step you take..."

His husky voice was coming from speakers which seemed to be cleverly hidden within the walls. She felt good, but her discomfort refused to go. Her body had started to develop cramps. She tried to call out, but it was useless as all she could manage was a muffled gasp. She had lost track of time but in a while she could feel her hands and feet being untied. She felt great relief as she stretched her body on the floor. She spread her legs and her hands to allow the strain from her earlier position to be released.

Her blindfold remained and her anxiety began to rise. She felt a pair of calloused hands grip her arms and raise her to a standing position. She was being led into another part of the room. Her knees touched some soft leather. She was gently pushed over and before she could hold onto anything she fell onto a leather couch. She felt her legs being spread and her cunt lips being tickled. She let out a small groan. It felt good. The touching continued but at the same time, each touch felt different. Sometimes it was rough and others it was soft and smooth. After a while her pussy juices began to ooze, first as a trickle and then a steady flow.

It wasn't much but she did feel horny and felt the need of a good climax. She now began to raise her waist to meet the touch and was disappointed when it stopped altogether. Her blindfold was removed with a single swift motion and as she peered into the room, she could see many faces, some of whom were familiar. Her gag, too, was removed now as she gawked around for a while.

There was applause and some laughter. Embarrassed she tried to cover herself, when Lincoln walked to her and covered her body with a large bath towel. He told her to go to the adjoining bathroom where she could find her clothes and get dressed. She nodded and clutching the towel even more firmly walked to the bathroom at the end of the room.

Once inside, she looked at herself in the large mirror. Her face and a mark around her cheeks where the leather straps had wound around just a few moments ago. Her inner thighs were still streaming the juices from her cunt. She ran her hands over them meaning to wipe them. Then changing her mind she walked to the showers and stood under the streaming jets of warm water as it washed away her exhaustion.

When she came out and flopped onto the couch, she passed out. When she woke up, the room was empty except for Lincoln, who was slouched on a soft couch in deep sleep. She got up and walked up to his side, ran her hand over his forehead, bent down and planted a kiss on his lips. The kiss woke him up and he looked up at her and smiled.

"Hungry?" he asked her, setting aside all protocol of the relationship. She nodded and smiled back. Lincoln looked relieved after having noticed that Katrina was comfortable. He held her waist and kissed her lips, gently and then they walked out of the room, trooped upstairs to the dining area.

The table had several porcelain plates of cold cuts, salads, cheese and slices of whole wheat bread. Nodding towards the table, Lincoln told Katrina to help herself. She looked at him, her eyes inquiring if he, too, would have some. He shook his head saying that he had already eaten. Katrina took a plate, filled it with the tossed salad and found a place to sit and wolfed down the food. As she was eating, Lincoln asked her about her experience.

"I was a bit frightened at first but now I am quite comfortable," she said in a soft voice. "At any point, did you feel threatened or uneasy?" he continued to probe her. She shook her head without looking up. "Are you enjoying the feeling?" he asked her yet again. Katrina nodded her head vigorously and then looked up and smiled at him. She looked at his face as if asking – What next? "I have some work to do in town," he said, "I would like you to do some chores in the house while I am gone and I have asked Alisha to pick you up within the next hour or so. Here, keep this with you."

He threw a set of keys in her direction and quickly got up and walked away. Katrina could catch the keys as she was not expecting him to throw them at her and she also held her plate in the other hand. She was surprised at the abruptness of what had just happened and grimaced. Just then a tear rolled onto her cheeks and she burst out crying. Her sobbing stopped just as soon as it had started. She got up and began her cleaning work. She could see the sunlight come over the lawn throwing shadows over it. She was almost done when she heard the doorbell ring.

It was Alisha, who greeted her with a warm hug. She looked at her, inquiring as to how she enjoyed the experience. Katrina told her everything and also that she had felt sad at the abruptness in which Lincoln had left the house without even a goodbye kiss. Alisha consoled her by saying that it was typical of his behavior. "He is rude sometimes," she said. She went on to tell Katrina about Lincoln's behavior towards his slaves. Katrina was curious as to how she had known about all this. "I am his slave too, except my role is limited to helping you to get trained well," she said slowly.

Katrina was dumbstruck as she looked at Alisha in wonderment, at her patience and yielding to the situation. "If you're ready, we could leave and we can talk some more on the wa,y" she said and Katrina readily agreed as they walked towards the car. While in the car, Alisha gave yet another shocking piece of news. She told Katrina that Lincoln was her husband and they had been married for t long years.

She came to be his slave during that period and she has since then obeyed everything that he asked her to do. She told her that she was very happy in her role and did not even feel jealous at the prospect of Katrina taking her place by his side. Soon enough the car pulled up at hugged Alisha tightly and then without any word, walked back to the house.

4 THE PASSION OF SUBMISSION 3: THE DOMINATION

It was 6 a.m. when she went off to bed. Katrina had been up the whole night putting together data for her uncle's business. The business had flourished thanks to Katrina's homegrown relationship management techniques. She had started with a casual call to a customer just to confirm the arrival of a worker from the facility. The customer in turn had taken to conversing with Katrina, praising the promptness of the effort and how it had resolved her leaky roof problem. Thereon, Katrina took up to calling all her customers just to inquire about the quality of work.

The client, on hearing her sweet voice responded well. Soon, word spread and business boomed. Uncle Antonio was way too happy at his niece's initiative and also increased her salary to $600 a week. Encouraged by this, she had purchased an iPad which could connect to the internet and to the central system at the office. This system helped not only to generate bills on time but to also record the inventory in the warehouse. This had resulted in tremendous saving of time and funds that Antonio was actually considering the idea of retiring and handing over the reins of the business to Lincoln and Katrina.

For the systems, Katrina had sought the help of an old classmate, Kevin, whom she had chanced to meet at the local mall. Kevin was a geek in school and had remained one. It was his IT knowledge of which had brought to Los Angeles. He was now a director of Technical Operations at CIBCO Inc., a warehousing company. Over coffee at the food court in the mall, Katrina had mentioned to him about her work and casually broached the subject of the use of technology in it. Kevin had enthusiastically come forward with some great ideas. Katrina triggered something in him and he was prepared to create simple software for the business, free of cost. All he needed was for Katrina to prepare a database at her end. It was pretty late and she had failed to see the numerous missed calls on her cell phone. There were three calls from Alisha and one from Lincoln.

She had called up her Master first and shared the latest developments with him. Lincoln seemed less interested but listened patiently. He agreed to help her if the need arose. Katrina had told Lincoln most of the details except for one. She had promised Kevin that she would spend one night in bed with him, and this was what she kept out of her conversation with her Master. It did worry her but she had realized that what Kevin had to offer would benefit the business in many ways. For this, she would have to reward him if not by any other means, at least from what she could give him. Kevin had been dumbstruck by Katrina's offer but who was he to refuse? He had only dreamt and spent nights imagining scenarios where he would merrily copulate in his own way with this beauty.

Reminiscing that particular night, Kevin would often sit on his deck chair, located on his balcony overlooking the city of Los Angeles, a glass of Chianti in hand. It was midweek, he had had a very exhausting day at work and had just stepped into the shower. Suddenly his doorbell had rung twice as if the person was in a hurry.

"Coming," he shouted and wrapped a towel around his middle, water dripping from his forehead. His jaw had dropped; standing at his front door was Katrina.

A tight shirt carving out her breasts and an equally tight pair of low waist denim jeans completed her attractive figure. She had applied a maroon shade on her lips and this enhanced her sexiness even more. All Kevin could do was just stand and stare. Little did he realize that he was at his front door, with just a large Turkish towel wrapped around his middle, his mouth open.

"Are you going to ask me inside?" asked Katrina.

"Oh yes! I am sorry, please come in" he muttered incoherently. He stepped aside and as she passed he took a deep breath inhaling her perfume. He followed as she walked and sat on the leather couch. Kevin's house was a three room affair. It had a living room, a bedroom and another spare room which had a low bed. His kitchen was sparse as also the living room except for a large wall mounted television screen, and a Sony PS3.

"Were you in your shower?" Katrina asked. Kevin just nodded. He did not even object as she took off her shirt, unzipped her pants and started walking towards the bathroom. Now completely naked, she stood for him to enter the bathroom.

Instead, Kevin sank on his knees and held her well shaped buttocks digging his mouth into her vagina. Katrina giggled as she held on to the door frame and steadied herself. Kevin was stroking his tongue on her vaginal. Katrina sighed as she closed her eyes and took the moment to relinquish herself to this geeky man. She gently stroked his hair with her fingers and grunted as Kevin intensified his movements. Now she cupped her hands around his head and pushed his head in a rhythmic motion. She was about to reach her climax when he stopped and stood up nervously. His towel had slipped off and his cock now stood erect and hard as if paying homage to her dripping cunt. Katrina hid her disappointment and held Kevin's waist. "Do you want me to suck your cock?" she asked.

"Yes, yes please," he responded breathlessly. Katrina kneeled before him and held his cock lightly rubbing it and feeling the texture. The head was pink and looked very juicy as there was also a faint trickle of his pre-cum on it. She took it in her mouth and felt the delicious sensation sink into her mind. Kevin just closed his eyes and allowed Katrina to lead. She had held his scrotum in her hands and gently started to massage it. Her fingers felt for his prostate as she had heard that it was where the male G-spot was located.

Rubbing it now she could hear Kevin groan deeply a he lay his hand on her head. Katrina's head bobbed at a greater speed as she wanted to get into the shower. Just then Kevin stopped her and held her arms, raising her to stand. He bent low to kiss her but just managed to peck her lips. His hands travelled to her breasts and he reveled at massaging them ever so gently that it made Katrina giggle. He then led her into the shower.

The hot jets from the spout overhead brought some respite from the cold outside. Both could feel the relief as they clung to each other's bodies. Kevin nervously ran his hands over her breasts and admired them through the sheets of water.

"Like them?" asked Katrina, "Then take them," she said. Kevin bent over her breasts and took one nipple into his mouth. Sucking with delight, he had only imagined about he held a hand to surround the breast and coaxed his mouth to swallow the whole breast.

It was clumsy but Katrina let him feel good about it. She felt different as Kevin had started to squeeze her breast. He then moved his attention to the other breast. After he had his fill with both the breasts, he raised Katrina's leg and tried to insert is erect manhood into her steaming cunt. Katrina took his cock in her hands and guided it to her vagina and just as he felt the softness of her cunt he pushed it inside with one stroke. His cock slid inside the velvety vagina and he began to moan in pure ecstasy.

He may have stroked it a few times when he felt his load gather at the base of his penis. He cried out her name and Katrina moved him out of her cunt just as he shot off his cum over her naked body. It was quite a bit and she was surprised at the quantity. After a quick shower they both trundled off to bed. Within minutes, Kevin was in deep sleep leaving Katrina staring at his face and smiling. Later she kissed him and turned over her side to sleep. She woke up early and left, but not before putting down a small thank you note by his bedside table. That was the only time that they had had a physical relationship but their friendship grew stronger over each passing day.

Even Lincoln had started to look up to her and admire her businesslike approach. She had also convinced him into letting Alisha to be around as together they could attend to his needs. Katrina had, over the period of time, become more alert and sensible.

Katrina woke up to answer her phone. It was Alisha at the other end. Lincoln was to be going to New York for three days and he wanted Katrina to come over to his house and stay there while he was gone. Katrina knew that it would hamper her work but she relented as she would never refuse Lincoln's authority. She went and took a shower, then called Kevin to tell him about the development. Kevin told her not to worry as he would tackle the details from his side. That way, they would be in a position to roll out the new system well in time. She thanked him and got ready to leave for Lincoln's house. She called a cab to come over and waited outside her house. The cab arrived and she got in, giving the address to the diver. It was past lunch time and she was hungry.

She could call for a pizza once she arrived at Lincoln's house. She knew why he had wanted her to stay over at the house in her absence. She knew about Alisha's trepidation of staying alone and she was only too happy to be there for her dear friend. Alisha would never openly say this to Katrina, so she had divulged this matter to Lincoln. The cab stopped at the signal at the North Broadway when she saw a familiar face. He was crossing the road and getting into yet another cab which was parked at the curb.

The lights turned green and the cab

surged ahead before Katrina could recollect the face. She looked behind as both cabs ebbed away. Deep in thought now, she had failed to notice that her cab had pulled up at her destination. Returning to the present, she paid the cabbie and strode towards the door. Just as she was about to put the key into the keyhole, the door opened and Lincoln stood there to welcome her. He held her close and kissed her deeply as Katrina, too, put her arms around his neck. He released her and led her into the house.

"Hungry?" he asked her and knowing her answer, pointed to the table where steaming slices of pizza lay in the cardboard containers. Smiling at him walked briskly to the table and taking a plate tore a slice and began to gorge on it. Lincoln took out a bottle of Coke and kept it on the table for her.

He gestured that he was going to the bedroom to complete his packing. Katrina nodded at him just as Alisha stepped into the room. She stopped Lincoln in his tracks telling him that she had packed his bag and that he could relax.

Soon, a taxi arrived at the doorstep to take Lincoln to the airport. Lincoln went into his room and returned with his bag. He stopped by near Alisha, drew her close to him and kissed her. And then did the same to Katrina.

"Take good care of each other and be good while I'm gone," he said and quickly walked out of the house into the waiting cab. The women ran to the open doorway to take a last look at "their Master" before he left on his trip. Lincoln, on his part did not disappoint, as he looked out of the departing cab and blew both of them a kiss each and waved his hand, smiling at them.

The women waved back and then went into the house, shutting the door behind them. Inside in the cool confines of the house, Katrina finished her pizza and kept the plate in the kitchen sink. When she came back to the room she could hear Alisha sobbing softly. As she came into view, Alisha was lying on her stomach on the couch and was crying.

Concerned, Katrina approached her and gently laid her hand on her back. "Alisha, what's the matter?" she asked. "It's nothing, Katrina, nothing that could cause any concern to you" said Alisha. Running her hands through her straight hair, Katrina repeated her question. Alisha got up suddenly and walked up to the bathroom to wash her face as her makeup was ruined. She came back and sat by Katrina's side and held her hand.

"Had it not been for you being around, I may have ended my life," she said seriously.

"Why?" asked Katrina, surprised at this revelation.

"Lincoln has ruined my life over these years," she burst out in mild anger. "He has been pushing me to the extremes and this has had a telling effect on me," she continued. She said that he would beat her black and blue without any remorse, especially after he drank.

She raised her skirt and showed her the marks of hot iron branding just above her vagina. There was a clear "L" appearing on that part. "After you have entered his life, I have been saved from the dreadful condition," she said.

Katrina thought to herself that maybe soon, it would be her turn. She clasped her hands together and shut her eyes for a moment, deep in thought.

According to Alisha, during their earlier days together, Lincoln was infused with profound love and made her feel like a princess. Before their marriage, it was the common interest in BDSM which had brought them together and Lincoln, with his magnificent personality, had succeeded in drawing her close to him during those days they were in a "vanilla" relationship. It was only later that the relationship took an extreme turn.

It got even more intense after their marriage and from thereon it was slowly sliding downhill. Katrina pacified Alisha by saying that she would try to resolve the crisis as soon as Lincoln returned from his trip to New York. Katrina was also surprised that Lincoln had kept the reason for his trips under wraps from everyone. In fact Alisha told her too was not aware of it.

The following day, Katrina left early for work taking a cab and just as they were passing North Broadway, her eyes scanned the road ahead, hoping to catch a glimpse of the figure she had seen yesterday. She was certain that she would be able to see the face this time long enough for her to recall who it was. She found a fuming Uncle Antonio at the entrance of the office. He was angry at the abrupt Lincoln's departure to New York without any notice.

He was not even aware as to what was the nature of work which had taken him to New York. Katrina cooled him off and rushed inside her office to commence her day's work. Her phone was ringing noisily and she grabbed it even before sitting down.

"Antonio's Maintenance Services, how may I help you?" she spoke in a smooth calming voice. "Yes, I have called to inquire if you also handle rat infestation?" said the voice at the other end. It was a strong sonorous voice and yet again Katrina felt a certain kind of familiarity when she heard it. "Indeed, we do provide those services, and if you could give me your name and address, I shall depute one of our team members to see to the problem," she spoke in response. The voice across rattled out an address in the vicinity of North Broadway and immediately bringing back the same sense of familiarity.

Thanking the customer after taking down the telephone number, Katrina briefed her team about the details. She went on with her usual routine but the voice kept haunting her. It was a voice form the past and it was close to her, very close. She continued with her work during the day but something happened that afternoon that would change many things in her life.

A little after lunch she got a call from Alisha. She was frantic and her talks were gibberish. All she could clearly hear is "SHOT DEAD."

Why would Alisha call her up and say all this? She gave the phone to Uncle Antonio and asked him to speak as she could not make out much. Her heart sank as she saw the look of anguish on Uncle Antonio's face.

"Madre Mia," was all he could manage in his state. "Lincoln has been shot dead, and that was the police who called Alisha on the phone to inform her about it," he managed to say. Katrina's face grew ashen and she just could believe it to be true.

"Tell me it is not true Uncle Antonio, it cannot be true," she screamed. She immediately grabbed her purse and rushed over to Alisha. Alisha was at the gate crying profusely and she had held the gate post for support as Katrina came running out of the cab.

They both hugged each other and began to cry. Supporting each other, they staggered towards the house. Alisha then said in between her sobs that Lincoln had gone to New York to make a drug deal with one of his friends in LA.

Just when they were about to leave the meeting with the cache of drugs, the police had come in. Lincoln's counterparts had opened fire at the police in an attempt to escape. He and his friend had caught bullets in the crossfire and died instantly. Both of them had been consoling each other as dusk approached.

The phones had not stopped ringing off the hook with his friends and others from the BDSM community calling in offering their sympathies. Alisha had meanwhile brought out a bottle of wine and after taking a long swig offered it to Katrina.

They polished off the bottle in an attempt to numb themselves of the grief that had struck them.

The funeral was a simple affair but had drawn a large contingent of friends and people who knew Lincoln. Katrina and Alisha were inconsolable as the time came for them to sprinkle soil over the coffin. Later that day, as the all the guests had left, a lawyer had come forward and given his card to Alisha.

He had said that he would be visiting the next day to read Lincoln's will to her. It had now become clear to Alisha and Katrina as to why Lincoln had kept his visit a secret until then. He had known that they would have asked him the reason for the sudden visit to New York. All of his friends and acquaintances had been shocked at the revelation. A police officer from the local prescient had visited Alisha during the week to ask her questions about Lincoln's dealing. Even Uncle Antonio had received a call from the police.

The next day, at 10 a.m., the lawyer Mr. Jones came over and informed Alisha about the house, the cars, and his business partnership with Uncle Antonio was left to her. Alisha had insisted for the presence of Katrina and Uncle Antonio. Further, she also informed Mr. Jones about her decision to give one of the cars to Katrina. She insisted that even the house be made in both her as well as Katrina's name. This surprised Uncle Antonio as well as Katrina but they both knew better to question Alisha's deeds at this stage given her vulnerability. So as planned, Katrina moved into the house the very next day much to Alisha's relief. Alisha used to be a beautician and she was once the most sought after expert, working at an exclusive salon in the Santa Monica area.

Taking cue of her expertise, Katrina had suggested to her to start a Spa and a salon in the basement of the house. She promised her help, in whatever way possible. The very first thing to do was to find a good designer so Katrina began her hunt, scanning the internet, the newspapers and the magazines. She spoke to quite a few of them and even met some. But she wasn't quite happy with the outcome.

Then one day, she was on her routine calling up customers inquiring about the services the company had rendered. One such customer was unhappy that the gas used to hunt out the rats in his house had left a faint odor in some corners. The voice again, thought Katrina, was now very familiar but she could not place it.

Suddenly her mind travelled to distant Phoenix, Arizona. It was Javier, it had to be him. With some hesitation she risked a question. "Is that you, Javier?" she inquired. There was silence across the other end as she waited with a bated breath. "Yes, this is, who is this?" Katrina's heart leapt and she was dumbstruck for a few minutes.

"Hello? Hello?" asked Javier repeatedly. "It is me, Katrina, from Phoenix," she spoke with a whisper.

"Katrina? You mean Aunt Kayla's Katrina?" he asked, surprised at the disclosure. Katrina was nodding feverishly as everyone was staring at her.

"Yes, yes!" she said excitedly. They were on the phone for at least an hour. After a long time, a big smile had lit up Katrina's face and she was on top of the world thereafter.

She could not believe her good fortune of meeting her heartthrob after all these years. She had invited him over to the house she now shared with Alisha. She had called up Alisha and given her the good news. Alisha had expressed her happiness over the development and told Katrina that she would cook for them. The news had been also brought her some relief from the grief of losing Lincoln. For Katrina it was much more than relief. It was rekindling of some enormous thoughts, thoughts of looking towards a bright future.

Katrina worked frantically during the afternoon with the hope that she could visit a salon close by and get a facial done. Then she remembered that she could always request Alisha to do it for her. She left office early that day and rushed home. Waiting for her was Alisha ready with all her creams and dabs. Within a couple of hours, Katrina's face bore a new look. The strain under her eyes seemed to have just disappeared. She quickly showered and put on a sheer black backless dress that she had picked up during one of the numerous shopping sprees she and Alisha had gone on.

Happy with her looks, she walked past Alisha a few times, emulating a fashion model. Alisha showered her with compliments and their laughter filled the room. So immersed were they that the doorbell went unheard the first time and it was only when it rang again that Katrina walked quickly to the door and opened it.

There in a pale yellow shirt, pleated trousers and black hair stood Javier, his lips beaming one of the brightest smiles the women had seen.

hugged him tightly. She kissed him on his lips, lingering a while and then released herself. Javier still held her waist with his left hand as his right held a bottle of Chablis, the white wine with a flinty taste.

He handed over the bottle to Katrina and walked alongside her as she led him inside the house. She introduced Alisha to Javier and as they talked amongst themselves Katrina went into the kitchen fetch the wine bucket.

On learning of their plans of setting up a spa and salon, Javier instantly expressed his desire to design and redo the entire house, all free of cost all to the delight of both the women. They stared at each other disbelief.

Alisha's phone rang and as she excused herself and went into the next room, Katrina went and perched her petite buttocks right on Javier's lap. She then planted a warm wet kiss on his lips, sucking his lower lips openly. Her kiss stirred up his loins as she could feel movement against her behind.

She laughed lustily, clearly indicating her desires to this gorgeous man. Javier chuckled easily and looked at her eyes. How she had changed since the last time he had laid his eyes on her. She looked fuller and even more confident than the wiggly, restless girl he had known for a few days. Alisha came back and announced that she would be leaving to go to her friend Murielle's residence for the night as she had organized a get together of all her friends.

"As it is you two may have a lot catching up to do, I shall leave you both alone to enjoy the night," she smiled and with a fleeting glance left through the door.

Javier kissed Katrina once again but this time he took the lead, rolling his tongue deep inside her mouth and then closing his mouth over both her lips, letting it go with a distinct puckering sound. His hands travelled over her outer thighs up to her waist and he raised his eyebrows at not being able to feel any fabric as his hand came over a naked buttock.

"Mmmmmm! Delicious," he exclaimed in sheer delight. Katrina's eyes had closed and she was reveling in the feeling of ecstasy rising inside her body up to her breasts tickling her nipples to come erect. Without hesitation, Javier pulled down the strap of the dress and stared for a while at her breasts. Then raising her a bit his mouth dove to gently pucker at her nipple and then taking the full breast in his mouth. He sucked hungrily.

Katrina looked down at the mop of hair and ran her hands over it likening a mother who could be suckling her child and moaned. Javier's mouth had a magical effect on Katrina as she pushed her breasts towards his face. His hands had now moved to between her legs and he used two of his fingers to rub her pussy lips which were wet and mushy with juice. He brought the fingers to his mouth and sucked at them, which drove Katrina even crazier as she began to buckle at his touch. Javier stopped now and moved Katrina away from his lap to kneel between his legs. He just sat there, legs spread wide and arms flung over the couch's backrest.

Katrina did not have to be told any further as she immediately stripped off her clothes and naked kneeled before him. She quickly unbuckled his pants and tore at his "banana hammock" front, bringing forth an engaging sight of his huge bulbous cock. She was speechless as she kissed the head first before gobbling it into her mouth.

She began stroking it and moaning at the same time,an indication that she was enjoying herself. Javier pulled out the pins on her hair, with both his hands he firmly gripped them. He guided her stroking and had her slow the pace. Katrina took the opportunity of nibbling at the sides of his foreskin sending bolts of pleasure to Javier's body as he shook.

With her hand she gently massaged his prostate enhancing his bliss even more. Javier had moved the toe of his shoe right into a position from where he could clearly insert the bronze tip inside Katrina's wet cunt. She wiggled wildly trying to match the motion. Just then Javier stopped her and stood up. He motioned her to stand by the couch, spread her legs wide and hold the backrest for support. Katrina did as she was told as her heart hammered with renewed rapture. She waited with bated breath as Javier pulled down his trouser and guided his enormous erection inside her waiting cunt.

Katrina drew in her breath deeply as she felt the engorged cock enter her succulent pussy. She could feel the tightness and even felt a little pain, but she closed her mind to it and waited. Javier had been gentle as he knew that the sudden intrusion would not be pleasurable and he stopped and began stroking gently not taking it deeper than the limit he knew. Katrina now started to whimper softly at each stroke and her point of no return began to emerge. Javier's stroking was unhurried and he maintained a steady pace allowing Katrina to enjoy the moment. Just then he heard her buckle and shake as the first orgasm hit her and she screamed loudly flailing her hand behind trying to touch Javier.

He stopped and turned her over, laying her on the thick rug on the floor. His cock was well marinated with her pussy juice and once again he slipped inside her cunt with ease. Now his movements in at a brisk pace and his hands were on her well rounded breasts. Squeezing her breasts, he found euphoric joy which was beyond his erotic experience and the movement of the fucking made it even more delightful. He had held back his ejaculation a little while longer, wanting Katrina to come too. It was then that she began to flail her head from side to side and her grip on his forearm grew tight.

Both exploded at the same time and felt the harmony like the fireworks on the Fourth of July. Javier lay on her body kissing her on her face and breasts lovingly as a smile lit up Katrina's face. Her journey of submission had finally reached its destination as she whispered in his ears.

"Will you be my Master for life?" she said.

5 WET AND HUNGRY

The storm that had dumped buckets of rain on the region finally waned, the downpours thinning to a drizzle as Anita walked to the window of her apartment. The Langham Court was part of a brownstone legacy, which a dear friend from college had recommended, going so far as to give Anita's name to the landlord of the three-story apartment. Spacious and elegant, the décor was minimalistic, yet homey. Anita had fallen in love with the place the moment she had set eyes on it.

She had spent the last hour satisfying her sexual urges with a vibrator. She had spent the time awash with the sweat as she spasmed, her torso raised above the couch and her legs spread wide while mind-blowing orgasms made her scream. That had gone on until she had collapsed on the floor.

"My God," she uttered breathlessly before rousing herself up to make a cup of coffee.

She had left for work as usual that morning despite the bitter weather, but there was no one, not even the regulars, visiting the library that day so she had called her superior and requested permission to call it a day.

Walking past the Upper Crust Pizzeria, she decided to pick up her favorite margarita pizza. At the last minute, she decided to purchase a Greek salad with chicken for her dinner as well, just to avoid going back out into the weather.

As she stood there looking down from her window, her eyes chanced upon a strapping tanned figure, clutching two bags, leaping out of a taxi, and jumping over the shrubs which lined her building's porches. The figure looked familiar, and her heart missed a beat when she recognized him.

"Oh my God!" she heard herself saying.

It was Chris Martin, her teen heartthrob. She smiled as she felt a tug between her legs. She looked in the mirror to straighten her hair and could not help blushing. All of a sudden, she composed herself.

"What business does he have with me now?" she asked herself. "Alright, he was a friend, but that's all."

She surprised herself when she sprinted to the door and waited. The doorbell did not ring. What if he had come to some neighbor's home and not hers? Disappointed at the prospect, she dropped into her favorite chair that sat by the windows. Almost instantly, her doorbell chimed. Leaping out of the chair, she went to the door and peered through the peephole at a tanned face covered in stubble and bright mischievous eyes. She realized that her heartbeats had increased. She could swear that she almost heard the heavy thunder of her heartbeat. She turned the doorknob and opened it.

"Ta dah!" Chris shouted.

Before she could react, he had her in his arms kissing her cheeks. Although she was thrilled, Anita did not show it. She smiled warmly and held him tightly.

This was the first time she had hugged a man in a year. Her engagement with Victor, the banker, had broken after she had walked into his apartment only to see him fucking his secretary when he was supposed to meet her for lunch. She had been aghast at the sight of Victor's erect cock sending jets of semen all over the carpet in the bedroom. She had thrown the ring in his face and scurried out of the house.

Leading her childhood friend into the house, she smiled as she looked at his square face. He looked tired, yet his eyes were a sparkling, emerald green.

He put his hand on her shoulder. "So, how is my best friend doing?" he said lightly.

"Your friend is doing pretty fine but is really surprised at your showing up like this after such a long time," she responded trying to sound sarcastic but without success.

"Yes I agree, it was a surprise,e" he said seating himself. "I was deep inside the jungles of the Congo Basin on UNICEF assignment to tend to the children of the local tribesmen suffering from malnutrition."

He was a doctor working with UNICEF's medical team. He began to explain, telling her that he had gotten a call from his aunt Betty's neighbor. Betty had passed away and that the funeral was to take place in the following week. He had rushed to get here early enough but had completely forgotten that his apartment building was going through a renovation. "Where else could I go but seek help from my dear friend, Anita?" he turned to her with a smile.

"Anita, could I stay with you for a few

days?" he asked.

"Sure, you can."

"Why don't I freshen up and then hit the sack, since I have had a long trip? I can make myself comfortable on that couch if you don't mind."

"I have a spare room Chris" interjected Anita. "You can move your luggage in the same room, too," she added. Moving to the storeroom, she pulled out fresh towels and handed them to Chris.

In less than a half hour, her guest was snoring softly. Anita watched his chest rise and fall from the door of the room. When was the last time she had seen him she wondered as she returned to the living room to watch some TV. Even after an hour, she was not able to settle onto any program to watch.

It was dark outside, and the streetlights threw a gleam across her bedroom ceiling. The light was the same, yet it looked different. In her bed, Anita stared at it as her thoughts flew into the past. Chris had been her friend, hero, mentor and a great person to hang around with. Anita looked up to Chris as her knight in shining armor, even though they grew up together and he decided to take Betty, her bitter enemy, to the prom. She hid all her feelings about it, not telling him for fear he would not care. He just waved back at her when they passed each other.

Her hand slid inside her panties, while the past plays in her mind, spreading the lips of her pussy, and her finger started to rub her clit, slowly and then faster. She finger fucked her pussy. She was so damn wet! And her creamy juice made her crave more. She soon couldn't take it any longer, she let out a moan and boom! she came. Just the thought of Chris really made her cum. That's how much she wanted him all this time. Eyes still open, she let out a tender sigh and hoped that one day he could have sex with Chris. A frown and then a smile appeared on her face. "It is Chris after all," she said to herself. He would never be hers, and he was there just because it was convenient. With this thought, she slipped into a deep slumber.

The outside sounds awakened Anita. She stepped out, and what she saw took her breath away. Standing next to the coffee maker was Chris in his boxer shorts whose front formed a neat tent. By the look of it, his penis was rock hard, and he did not seem to be bothered by it.

Anita cleared her throat merely to announce her presence... Chris turned around, oblivious to his enormous erection, and greeted her with a "coffee?" She nodded and smiled shyly, wanting to get closer so she could gorge on that wonderful member inside his boxers. She was no less enticingly dressed. Her cleavage peeked from within her parted gown, and it caught Chris's attention. She stepped closer to him as he handed her the coffee mug. She took a sip and nodded in approval. Chris smiled, and then she found him looking at her face. He put his mug on the table and advanced towards her. He took her hand and looked at it then took the mug off her other hand as he lowered his mouth to kiss her neck. Anita let out a moan. Chris moved the thin fabric away from her waist and gently rubbed her slender waist. The result was magical as Anita drew her body closer to his, almost touching their torsos. She felt a hint of his hardness and let out a soft whispery squeal.

Chris began to kiss her moist, hungry lips. He started to suck her lower lip softly as his hands travelled to Anita's buttocks, exposing them as he raised her gown. His chiseled hand felt good, and she moaned over and over again. Her pussy leaked a little juice that slid down on her inner thigh, tickling her a bit. She lowered

Chris's boxers and gasped as her hands gripped his thick cock. She stroked the hardness of it as Chris let out a lazy moan, taking a moment to relish the pleasure of her strokes. Then almost like an animal that had been hungry for days, he picked her up and rushed to the leather couch in the middle of the living room. Spreading her legs, he volunteered a brief look at his region of interest. The pink lips of her hairless vagina were twitching. The wetness had left a sheen on it that made it even more enticing... Without a thought, Chris plunged his mouth to cover her mound. Then he inserted his tongue into her cunt, as deep as it could get and brought it out as if savoring it. He ran his tongue along the length of her pussy seeking her throbbing clitoris. Once found, he began sucking it, making it almost unbearable for her to stay still. Anita moaned loudly without a care if her voice would be heard out of her apartment. She was almost at her peaking crescendo when Chris stopped and pulled himself up.

He drew himself up and brought his cock close to her mouth. Anita grabbed it with both her hands and took him into her mouth hungrily, sucking the hardness while stroking it with her hand. Chris closed his eyes and raised his head high toward the ceiling. Without a word, he pulled himself out her wet mouth and poised himself for the final plunge. He thrust his hard cock, deep into her velvety wet and waiting cunt.

"Yes!" she cried as she wrapped her legs around his waist. She could feel that each thrust and that tug raging deep inside began to raise its intensity of twitching. She drifted into a haze of lust feeling each stroke in unison of her movement. Then without warning, both of them shuddered.

Loud moans, which may have heard right across the quiet neighborhood, broke from both of them. Anita felt her cunt throbbing as Chris' semen gushed into her.

She held him as he collapsed onto her body.

Chris kissed her softly, and she returned his kisses, and he finally spoke: "this was long overdue, don't you think?"

She smiled. "From now on, you will stay here by my side."

He looked at her face and nodded,. The weak sunlight played on the window of the apartment as the lovers kissed in celebration of their coming together.

6 A PRELUDE TO INDULGENCE

It was Irma's first day at work and it was a new experience for her. She had been married two years ago to her childhood sweetheart Aston and their lives were fulfilled. Then one day her life had come apart. Aston had been having an affair and one morning during breakfast, he announced that he was leaving their home and the town to live with his girlfriend. Irma's dreams were shattered. Coming from an immigrant Polish family, she had always looked to being sheltered from life's turmoil.

Her parents had been granted asylum since her father had fled from that country and from political persecution. That was ages ago and Irma was their only child. She was born late when the couple had nearly given up hope of having any child. She was called a miracle by her relatives and family friends. Her father, Ivan Wozniak, was a liberal thinker, but her mother was a meek, fearful, and weak woman. The couple's experiences in their own country had left her scarred for life.

Yet, with her father's brave and robust outlook, she had lived a pleasant, undisturbed life in the US. Irma's outlook towards life had emerged out from her mother's shadows as well as her father's audacity. She had grown up to be an exceptionally attractive woman with flawless skin and sharp features. Her body was what men would love to drool over, and without her even wanting to, she always attracted male attention wherever she went.

She had met Aston when one day when their town had been battered by unprecedented rain and they had found themselves marooned in a café. They were both in college, but he was older.

The café was located on a higher part of the town and it had been crowded. The lower regions were flooded and there was complete chaos. It was Aston who had taken charge and calmed the crowd inside the café. Later he had waded through the flooded waters to fetch help, and during that time, the water, too, had receded. Later, he had volunteered to take Irma to her house, where her parents thanked him. After several coffee dates, Irma felt that she was ready to follow the man of her dreams. She blindly followed Aston's life closely and found herself completely under his influence. Their wedding was not so dramatic and was attended by their families and close friends. Soon enough, in yet another tragedy, Irma lost both her parents one after another due to illness.

That was three years ago, and now she was without any direction. She slipped into depression. Her only anchor in life had left her in a lurch, and she was now lost. Her close friend Norma went to her home one day as she had not been responded to her calls. She was shocked to see Irma's condition and immediately had taken her to the nearby clinic. Later she took Irma to her own house, and after a few days of talking, her condition had improved. She had returned home and settled down. She had some savings but had realized that she would have to find work to survive and lead her own life. Her naiveté had rendered her helpless from asking for any financial support from Aston. She had responded to an advertisement as a financial assistant and had succeeded in her interview with the panel with her knowledge of number-crunching strategies. It had been her first job and she had even lost sleep during the night fore due to her nervousness.

Finally, the day had arrived and she made her way to the bus stop as her place of work was nearly an hour's commute from her place. Waiting at the bus stop, she was lost in thoughts of how she was going to deal with the day. Just then, the bus she was waiting for arrived and ground to a halt at the stop. There was just enough space for a few people to board it, and she was one of them. With some requests and urges, she managed to make space for herself between two seats.

There was standing room and she held on to the bar sticking out of the wall of the bus. This part did not have any glass and it was quite comfortable for her. There was a middle-aged man seated on the lone seat. He seemed too involved in reading his papers that he did not notice Irma's presence. The bus lurched forward and was picking up speed when she felt a hand rubbing against her inner thigh. Now as she was facing the front of the bus, there was no way of knowing whose hand it was. She pushed herself forward and the top edge of the seat in front of her touched her crotch area. Again the hand moved under her skirt, this time right up to the top nearly touching her pussy lips.

She felt a tingling sensation at the pit of her stomach and pushed her torso as much as she could towards the seat in front of her, and this time her pussy lips touched the metal of the top edge of the back seat. She was standing in such a position that no one could have noticed what was happening and she knew that too. It had been quite a long time since she had any sex, and this was emerging as an opportunity, but it was embarrassing for this shy and submissive woman. At first, she fought the urge as the touching was sporadic. But after a while, the hand kept up the pressure on her cunt lips, sending pulses of pleasure through her body.

It was getting more and more enticing, but she feared being discovered. The journey was going to be a quiet and long one, and she began to wonder how long this torment was going to go on. Now, the hand had pried open the panties from below and was touching her raw skin exactly underneath at the beginning of her pussy. It tickled as a faint moan escaped her lips. She had clasped the leather strap above her head, and her grasp firmed up a bit tighter that the skin of her hand turned pale. She shut her eyes to relish the moment and instantly opened them when she realized that she was on a bus. The hand had become bolder and had started tickling the insides of her now-wet pussy as she let out yet another moan. Her senses had started to soar as this was an experience in itself for a timid woman like her being abused in public.

The fingers were now doing a jig inside her cunt and were touching her clitoris as her breathing started to become deliberate. She could even listen to her heartbeat and the pulsating twitches in her pussy was becoming unbearable. Sometimes the fingers had managed to go right up to her G-spot as she had started to buckle under the assault. "Oh my God!" she exclaimed silently as she experienced a different feeling within her.

She was lost in her own world as everything else just began to vaporize around her. Just then the hand stopped and it was pulled out. She felt a jerky push as the owner made his way through the crowd, and that's when she had managed to catch a glimpse of the person. It was the same serious-looking gentleman who had his attention riveted to his newspapers when she had boarded the bus earlier. Her lips had a pout and her eyes were wide as she saw him smiling at no one in particular, passing her and getting off at the stop.

She could have never been defensive as that was not in her nature. But she enjoyed every moment. Something had been triggered inside, and it had kept her titillated until the end. Why was all this happening to her? What was it that made her so vulnerable, and why was it that she was savoring it? She made a mental note to talk it over with her close friend Norma.

Finally she was at her office where she was directed to her desk. She liked everything she saw the moment she sat at her desk. Her face lit up into a smile, which hadn't happened in ages. Just then the phone at her desk rang. She hesitated to pick it up at first but then picked it.

It was Juliette, her boss's secretary, asking her to come into his office and giving her directions since the office was situated on two floors. As she walked to the stairwell, she felt the remnants of the moistness from her earlier experience drip out onto her panties, and she became self conscious.

While going up the stairs, she thought about those earlier moments and surprised herself with a faint smile. Somehow she grew more confident at the thought, so much so that she did not find it necessary to go to the washroom to clean her cunt. It was as if she dared to do something she would have otherwise dreaded to do earlier. She knocked on the door which said David Brandon, Jr. and opened the door slightly. Juliette greeted her warmly and shook her hand.

"Go right in, as he is expecting you." Nervous now, she made her way through the soft beige carpeted floor and opened the door to David's cabin.

"Come in, Irma. Welcome to Brandon and Frazier's Fund Management. We are all glad to have you on board," said David warmly.

It was only then that she realized that there were three others sitting in the large office, overlooking the bay. She nodded as she was being introduced and shook hands with all four men before finally taking her seat in the vacant chair in the middle of David's nod.

David then handed her a sheaf of papers from a folder and asked her opinion. The papers contained investment opportunities for one of their clients. Irma quickly skimmed over the sheets one after the other, and then looking up, she said, "None of these will suit the client's return on investment." This statement stunned everybody in the room. She pointed out that the oil prices were likely to rise and during that period, if the investment was going to be made in the oil companies, it would be just parking the funds with no real value coming out of the deal. She suggested that it would be best if they looked up investing in IT-related successful startups, which could fetch rich dividends within a short period.

Brimming with confidence and some wickedness, she even thought of telling them that she was still dripping with pussy juices and would love to have any one of them to shove their fingers in her cunt to see that she was telling the truth. The thought shocked her and she immediately sat up. The men looked at each other and began to nod their heads in agreement.

A big smile came upon David's lips as he nodded at the others, beaming with pride.

"I shall have a surprise for you by evening, my dear Irma," he said.

The meeting concluded after he had defined her role and given her some more files to take with her. At the end of the day, Irma was surprised as David had come to her side.

"I have come here to inform you that your paystub will be reading a figure of $5,000 more than what was agreed in our contract, and that's not all. I have asked Martha, from administration, to help you get your driving license so your commute to work and back is much better," he said.

Irma just could not believe her good fortune as too many good things were happening to her just within that one day.

Irma showered and went to bed without having any dinner. She was too excited and had spent a long time in the bathroom to look at her body. She had never felt so eager in all these years. Earlier she had lived in the shadows of her parents and seldom had any erotic thoughts entering her mind.

Then it was Aston, who had been more of a hero than a real-life soul mate. She trod on a path on which he had walked, and even in bed she was being used as a sex object. Hence, she had never discovered her own sexual needs. It was now blooming like a flower in spring.

She ran her hands all over her body, but this time she was visualizing the experience not through her own mind but that of the stranger in the bus. She was hoping to get him to touch her yet again tomorrow.

With these thoughts, her hunger had vanished and she just settled for a glass of warm sweetened milk and went to bed. She tried closing her eyes and found that she was restless. She got up and tore all her nightclothes from her body; although it was a bit nippy that night, she wanted to sleep naked. Her hands travelled to her thighs as she spread her legs and slowly brought them to her cunt.

"Oh my God! I'm wet again," she said to herself as she gingerly rubbed her pussy lips. Her nipples had become hard and a strange, sweet pain was emitting from them. She pinched her nipples, gently rubbing her fingers together, and felt a gush of juice flow out of her vagina.

She worked her fingers with a smooth mechanical motion, which elucidated her hunger for release. It began to intensify as the seconds turned to minutes, and soon her fingers began to move faster and she lifted her waist higher as it met the ever-evading fingers. The faster her motion got, the more intense her eagerness to have an orgasm became. She felt her body shudder and her legs wrapped around her hand, her other hand squeezing her breasts together. She let out a howl as she had a powerful orgasm.

She had never ever had an orgasm before and had only known such sensation from her friends. But this time she felt it happen. Her bed sheet was slightly stained but that was not a bother for her now. Within a few minutes, she was lost in her slumber world.

The next day, she woke up and got ready as fast as she could, but this time she wore her shortest skirt, which came up to her knees. Just to feel good, she even left two of her top buttons open so that her ample cleavage showed up. She came to the bus stop and waited impatiently for the bus to arrive.

There was a crowd at the stop as usual since it was the peak time. No sooner did the bus come, she clambered onto it and moved towards the same position she had taken yesterday. Just as she was about to move into the corner, she noticed that the seat behind had been taken by an elderly lady and the stranger was standing just beside the seat.

It may have been that he offered his seat to the old lady as a common etiquette. Meekly she stood facing the front of the bus so that she could avoid the eyes of the stranger.

She was then lost in her thoughts about her day at work. Her breasts had also become a point of admiration from the other travelers as they all got an eyeful. For some reason, it did not seem to bother her as she continued looking towards the front of the bus. It was only when she felt an arm going around her waist did she come back from her thoughts. She refused to look at her side, not even to look as to who was holding her waist. The hand felt relatively smooth through her dress, but it did wake up her senses. She began to feel as dizzy as she had felt yesterday. But she held on to the strap over her head. Now the place where she stood was a step below while the entire bus was sitting or standing on a raised area, except for the lone seat behind her.

It was then that she had realized that "her stranger" had taken the seat and he had held the newspaper high enough to shield his hand from the sight of the other standees in the bus. He was taking his hand higher towards her exposed area of her breast since her right hand was raised to hold onto the strap.

There was no way that she could lower her hand to protect her breast from being touched. The stranger's hand went over to cover her whole breast, and she could also feel the touch of his skin on her exposed part.

She let out a sharp breath as he touched her, knowing how she would feel. The stranger's right hand was now prying open the small gap between the short sleeves, and in doing so, Irma felt the fingers touch the skin of her breast and this was creating tightness in the pit of her stomach. The stranger had managed to move his hand completely to encompass her whole breast, including the nipple. The wetness between her legs began to increase and so did the patch on her panties. The pressure of the stranger's hand on her breast was even as he used his fingers to feel the softness. For some reason, Irma did not feel violated but relished the feeling, and this sense of enjoyment increased as the bus navigated through the morning traffic.

Suddenly, the hand came off and she knew that "her stranger" would be getting off. Just then she saw him pass her without even a backward glance. She smiled to herself and waited for her destination to come. Arriving at her workstation, she was settling down when her phone rang.

This time it wasn't Juliette, but David himself asking her to come over to his office. As she knocked, she heard him asking her to enter. Inside she saw another woman, Martha, waiting for her. David completed the formalities of introducing both the women, and Martha brought out some papers for Irma to sign. She gave the papers a quick go-through before attesting them with her signatures.

Martha told her that she had arranged for the driving school instructor to pick her up from her home and she could drive down to the office; this would enable her to get used to the traffic and her driving lessons would be fruitful, too. Irma thanked Martha for being so considerate, and she also thanked David for what he had done.

Her grip on his hand was firmer and it was then that David had noticed something different in Irma's looks. She seemed vibrant and her face seemed to carry a glow which had been missing earlier on. This was a revelation to David as he had been recovering from a recently fought bitter divorce case, and it was as if his human instinct had opened a window of hope for him.

His heart leapt with joy and he suddenly seemed to like this woman's presence. He was so lost in his thoughts that he failed to realize that the phone at his desk was ringing. Juliette had called to remind him of his luncheon meeting. He was in half a mind to ask Irma to join him for the meeting but then thought otherwise. He excused himself and left for the meeting, while Martha and Irma completed their discussion. The change in David's behavior had not gone unnoticed by Irma as she saw some spark that she could not place.

That afternoon, during the lunch break, Irma went to the nearby deli and she was happy to see Juliette at one of the tables. She waved at her and Juliette asked her to join her.

"Do you come here often?" she asked her.

"Not really. I drop in when I feel like having a cheeseburger," Juliette replied.

"Tell me something, Irma. I noticed some sparkle in David's eyes just as he was leaving for his meeting earlier this morning after having met you. What happened in his office?" she inquired.

"I'm not sure exactly what you mean, but yes, he did seem different since we last met," said Irma.

It was then that Juliette told her about his divorce and how bad it had affected him. She told Irma as to how his ex-wife had stormed into the office and ridiculed him just so that he would pay for her trip to Paris with her so-called male friend. Irma was shocked at what she was being told and in the back of her mind she empathized with David as she saw them in the same boat. David was not to be seen the whole of that day.

From that day, Irma saw David as someone with whom she could relate to in some way or the other. She saw a bit of herself in him, or so she thought, and it lingered with her. The weekend was drawing near and everyone seemed to be happy at the prospect of breaking free from the tough routine that had been set at work. Irma had no major plans, and to top it all, her "stranger" seemed to have disappeared from the face of the earth. On her way to work on the third day, she had looked for him but didn't see him. This happened during the following days, too. She felt let down and mildly depressed and she grimaced. She knew that she would have to forgo her only sexual overture from the following week as she would be starting her driving lessons.

That morning, she had decided to give it all up and focus on her work. The weather had become unruly, with strong winds blowing. The weatherman on TV reported that a thunderstorm was to strike the city in the afternoon. But Irma had not paid much attention to it and had thought that if she kept her attention at her work, she would be able to keep her sanity, and so she promised herself not to divert her mind in any way.

She even refused a visit to the break room for a cup of coffee when Martha had called out to her. The office seemed abuzz with talks of the weather conditions getting worse by the hour. Irma had managed to complete most of her analysis of her client's investment plans. She was giving the finishing touches to her last paper when there was a loud crash. The French window at the far end of the floor had cracked after being hit by a metal bar from the railing outside. The bar seemed to have gotten loose due to some ill-fitting socket. The force of the wind had moved the bar out of its joint, and it had crashed into the glass. A delivery boy was hurt with the glass pieces flying. People ran about in panic until David came onto the floor and calmed them down.

An ambulance had been summoned and the boy was helped over to a chair. Someone had managed to get ice cubes which had been rolled into a piece of cloth, and someone held it to the boy's bleeding cheek. Irma sat on her chair, stunned by the development. She had seen the results of thunderstorms before since the town was prone to such natural calamities. But that was during her years in school and college, both of which were located close to her house.

Now she had started to panic and she had realized that she could be marooned in the office. The hour-long journey on the bus could present an imminent danger, or so she thought. She was so immersed in her own trepidations that she did not notice David's presence next to her desk.

"Irma? What are you thinking? You look worried," he ventured.

"Oh, it was just the thought of the weather which had me a bit worried," she said. "I wonder how I would manage the bus journey under such conditions," she continued.

David immediately put her fears to rest when he told her that she need not worry as she could spend her night at his home, just a few blocks away from the office. Irma sighed with relief and she thanked David for his compassion. It was later that she realized that it could be quite embarrassing if she did spend the night at his house.

Her shy nature made her even more

vulnerable to such a thought, but now she knew it was too late. She acknowledged David's gesture with a nervous smile and nodded at him.

When the city's administration began to announce through the local television station that everybody should return to the safety of their homes, David declared the office closed for the day. He had also asked female employees be escorted by any one male at least to a location nearest to their individual homes.

He had asked Martha to join them so he could drop her, too. Having made sure that all had left the office, he then drove to Martha's home, dropping her off there. From there, Irma and David continued their journey with some intermittent conversation, which mostly revolved around him asking her questions about her past. Little by little, David learned about Irma's miseries and he realized how cruel life could be. It was around 4:00 in the evening when David and Irma had reached his house. He casually laid his hand on her thigh and gently rubbed it.

It was a very unconscious move which was triggered by what she had just told him. Irma instantly felt a lurch in her heart and she also felt some moistness between her legs. Her sharp intake of breath did not go unnoticed.

However, she did not object to what

David was doing. In fact, she spread her legs slightly, allowing him to have further access to her vagina. She began to once again feel her "freedom" emerging as it had done earlier and now she did not wish to lose it. David looked at her sideways and saw her expression of desire. It was the same look he had noticed earlier and that was what had instantly attracted him to her.

He now knew that deep inside this serious-looking, shy woman was yet another side, trying to come out. Encouraged and also finding his expectations rising too, he inched his hand further up Irma's satin thighs. His hand had almost touched the edge of her panties when his house loomed at a short distance.

The neighborhood was an affluent one with every house having gates and driveways leading to the entrance. David's house was no less big and it spoke of the man's taste in everything good. It was a modern two-story structure.

Carved wooden balustrades greeted a visitor and the elevated entrance door also had some intricate work on its front face. He opened the door with his keys and, with his hand on her waist, led Irma into the house.

"In the corner, you will find a rack inside a closet, with some house shoes; get one of those for yourself and get comfortable," he told her.

Irma walked hesitantly towards the rack inside the closet and gingerly opened the door. She saw some beautiful shoes made of cloth, neatly placed in rows. She chose a light violet-colored pair that would fit.

As she turned back, David had trned on the TV and was watching the news. She walked towards the center of the room when David asked her to come towards him.

She came and stood in front of him at some distance. He drew her closer with his hands around her waist. As if mesmerized, Irma moved closer, keeping her eyes to the floor as she did not dare look up at David. He slid his hands up into her dress and ran them on her smooth buttocks. He locked his fingers on the edge of her panties and slowly pulled them down. Irma was breathless yet again and her anticipation began to mount. She came close and even helped David with her panties. Now she was naked below and felt shy and bit her lower lip and just then David looked at her face. "Wow," was all he said as he raised the hem of her dress to reveal her pussy. It was dripping wet and he brought his hand over it. He kept an open palm and slid it between her lips, dividing them with it.

He felt the moisture over his hand and

kissed her navel. Irma could not stand the sensation and she joined in by running her hand over his hair. She felt even better this time—better than she had felt when the stranger had her. She began to feel a sense of security, a sense of comfort.

She wiggled her body to get some enrichment from what David was doing. He removed her dress, leaving her only with her bra on, and Irma had not seemed to have realized it at all. She was moaning now as David used his hand expertly between her legs.

He had used his finger to touch her clitoris and was teasing it by gently rubbing on it in a circular motion. Then he did something which was least expected. He took off her bra and put his mouth over her voluptuous breast. "Oh, God," exclaimed Irma, and then he pushed his finger further up inside her pussy's passage to touch her G-spot. His incessant prodding on that spot began to push her to her limits. She had never reached this stage in all her sexual encounters, even with Aston. While Aston seemed to have used her as a sexual object, David was in a way worshipping the act and creating an erotic ensemble with the simple yet effective use of his hands.

Her breathing had started to come in short bursts now, accompanied by the sounds of her cries. Then, her orgasm hit her as her whole body shook like a dry leaf and only the whites of her eyes could be seen as her body curved backwards. She lost her balance, almost toppling over. David stuck his hand around her waist and held her firmly.

She regained her posture and opened her eyes dreamily. David stood up and held Irma close to his body. Her body was limp, except her hand which had gone around his neck. She smiled, eyes still dreamy, and brought her other hand to rub David's cheek.

She planted a light kiss on his lips to which David responded by pushing his tongue inside her mouth, just as his hard penis dug into her pussy. Irma took the cue and immediately pulled open his fly, opened his belt, and pulled down his underwear, which was already wet with precum. She put both her hands around his face and once again kissed him before kneeling in front of the erect cock. David's cock was slightly above the average size and Irma smiled as she took hold of it. She was orbiting a different galaxy at this moment.

She was very keen to explore her sexuality as she kissed David's cock head. She covered it with her wet mouth, nibbling it a bit and sending pulses of pleasure through David's body. He moaned and held her head between his hands and rubbed her hair, encouraging her along. Irma swallowed his cock as much as she could, trying her best not to gag on the large cock. She succeeded and that thrilled David, too.

He looked down at her and smiled, wanting to hold her as he began to believe that he had found his calling in Irma. He stopped her from sucking his cock and raised her to stand up. He held her close and hugged her as he began to feel an outburst of emotions within him. He lifted her lissome body and carried her effortlessly to his bedroom on the upper floor.

Once they were inside, he laid her gently on the bed and started to kiss her body all over starting at her head. When he reached her breasts, he paused for a moment. He looked at them, in awe of the size, the perfect well-rounded shape, and the perky nipples. He closed his mouth over one of the nipples as he felt it go hard.

David wanted to relish the sensations of those moments like a food connoisseur who would like to take his time over a dish. He then squeezed both her breasts and heard Irma cry out with pleasure.

He could also feel her cunt juice flowing as it dripped out, and he could feel some of it on his stomach. David moved his mouth to her navel and kissed it several times and finally hovered around her inner thighs. He rose and held his cock to guide it inside Irma's waiting pussy.

Irma lay on her back, with an expression on her face like that of a woman who was about to begin a limitless orgy. His hard manhood slid inside with a little effort and eventually he pushed hard and felt the warm velvety insides of her cunt enveloping his cock.

He began to move his cock in and out in a smooth and easy motion. His movements likened that of one rowing a boat on a quiet lake. At each stroke, Irma would sigh or moan as every time David moved in and out and his cock would graze her clitoris. Soon, David's movements increased and they became more like the pistons of a steam engine. He drove in his cock and pulled it out with more aggression as his balls slapped against Irma's buttocks, making a smacking sound. Even her breasts had started to move up and down in keeping with the thrusting movements of David's waist.

David reached out, held each of Irma's breasts, and squeezed them in his sexual stupor, and Irma's body began to shudder, indicating that she was coming closer to her climax. The next few moments saw an outburst as both David and Irma climaxed in unison. David immediately withdrew his cock, spraying and spurting his hot semen on Irma's stomach.

Finally he fell over her body, drained from the ordeal. Irma kissed him on his forehead and hugged him. David raised his head and looked down over Irma's face. He smiled and kissed her a few times on her lips.

"Promise me that you will never leave me, Irma," he said. Irma stroked his face, nodding. "I shall never leave you, my dear," she replied.

Irma had slept fitfully, with David's arm around her and her head rested on his shoulder. Next morning when David woke up, he could not find Irma by his side and panicked for a moment. "Where could she have gone?" he wondered. Just then his face brightened as he saw her coming into the room wearing his shirt and nothing else. In her hand she held a tray, which had a mug of steaming coffee, a tall glass of orange juice, and a plate with scrambled eggs, toast, bacon, and some baked beans. It was a wholesome meal, just like her future.

7 VEILED OBSESSIONS

Mabel woke up with a start as it was unusual for her morning alarm not to ring to herald her wake up hour. She rubbed her eyes and looked at the bedside clock in the dim light of the night lamp. She was relieved to see that it was only 4 a.m., which meant she could still sleep for two more hours. It had been a few days now that she would wake up at 6 in the morning and be at the bus stop before 6:30 a.m.

Her workplace, a bookstore, was located in Manhattan exactly an hour's drive from her Townsend Street, New Jersey, residence. And although the store would open at 9 a.m., she would be found loitering for a mere 30 minutes taking in the city's morning rush over coffee from a table in the nearby coffee shop.

Mabel, a 28-year-old arts graduate, lived with her elderly mother in the house she was born in. She had developed an interest in reading at a very early age, and this was what landed her the first job at the bookstore in New York.

Her employer had been quite impressed by her knowledge of books and had set his mind on making her the manager by the time she completed her first year. The time was drawing close, and Mabel ensured that she earned the position with her fortitude. Her primary interest had kept her so busy most of the time that she failed to make it up the social ladder in her neighborhood.

Barring casual greetings and salutations, she seldom exchanged much during her saunters to the supermarket or even during her return home. Although she was attractive with an hourglass figure, she dressed very simply so unless someone took a longer look they would fail to notice her beauty.

One such person who did venture to do so was 42-year-old retired war veteran Dick Smith. It had happened quite accidentally when Mabel had reached the bus stop just as the bus was about to leave. She had managed to jump onto the bus and was walking on the aisle towards her seat at the far end of the bus when suddenly a squirrel crossed the road forcing the driver to brake hard. This threw Mabel right on to the lap of Dick, who, with his presence of mind, held out his hands, preventing her from falling flat on the floor. Mabel thanked him and that is when he had a closer look at the beautiful face while one of his hands had unconsciously curled around one of her breasts. He held her for a while until she could regain her balance, and he got up so that she could go past him and sit on the next seat.

The driver apologized to all, though there were hardly any passengers in the bus. Mabel thanked Dick yet again as she settled in, and he was thinking of the beautiful lady sitting next to him. It had been raining outside and the only other passenger got off at the next stop. Now, they were all alone in the bus, and there was silence. The swaying of the bus had Mabel doze off a bit and she did not realize a faint touch on her right breast. It was there just for a second and she let it go.

There it was yet again and this time it was distinct as Dick leaned towards her side brushing his elbow cleanly on her softness. Mabel moved herself a bit towards the window just so that she could accommodate her co-passenger to be more comfortable. However, that was not to be as now his hand had crawled over her thighs sending goose bumps all over her body. She liked the sensation as she had never been touched like this before, but her coyness got the better of her so she kept quiet and held her gaze to the floor of the bus. Encouraged by her silence, Dick ventured even further now, raising her skirt baring her pale skin just above the elastic of her stocking.

There was a sharp intake of breath as his calloused hands dared to graze her thigh. She thought about a sideways glance to reprimand him in the act, but she just could not muster up enough courage to do so. The bus had just crossed the Brooklyn Bridge and was thundering past the toll booth when Dick got up from his seat to get off at the next. Just as the bus stopped Dick stole a glance at Mabel but she refused to meet his eyes. She very much wanted to look at him but somehow she just could not manage it. She hated the moment and knew that it would haunt her through the day.

Upon reaching the store, she found it locked and then realized her mistake. She had mistakenly set the alarm for 6 a.m. instead of 7 a.m. Looking around, she saw the coffee shop, where she goes during her afternoon break, had just opened. She decided to go and have a cup of coffee. As she sat down, she felt a bit uneasy between her legs. She walked into the ladies room and pulled down her panties. There was no red mark, but she could feel some secretion from her vagina as well as a mark on her panties.

Immediately, her mind raced to the instant in the bus. It was when the man sitting next to her had laid his hands on her thighs that she had begun to feel the wetness oozing out from her vagina. She was embarrassed now, and she could feel the heat in her cheeks. She was surprised to see herself blushing when she looked into the mirror. She had her coffee with a lot of deep thoughts, dark thoughts, as she would later confess to herself.

That evening, on her way back as she settled in her seat, her eyes searched the bus stop where the man had gotten off, but she did not see him. "Why am I doing this?" she thought to herself, chastising. The whole day had flown past with not much to do since it had been raining pretty hard that afternoon. The rains had stopped by evening and the air was fresh and cold. Mabel had walked briskly to her spot at the bus stop and looked around, quite conscious now ever since that morning's episode.

She was keen to know if people were

even looking at her, not that she was disappointed. She had boarded the bus and chosen to sit exactly at the same seat she had occupied earlier. The bus zoomed past the toll booth on its way towards its destination. Mabel reminded herself that she must change the alarm and set it right. That night, she went on through her usual routine, and just when it was time to go to bed, she took the clock and was about to change the alarm settings when she stopped. A smile appeared on her lips and she set the clock down without changing the settings. She went to bed humming a familiar tune.

The next morning, she was up at the ringing of the alarm. She got ready, only this time, she looked around in her cupboard for something different. She dressed and had her breakfast, trying not to hurry so that she could be there just a little before the bus arrived. She kissed her mother goodbye and ran down the road towards the bus stop. She could see the bus trudging along as sunlight had just broken into the horizon.

She was glad she was on time and waited for the bus in anticipation. The tingling sensation between her legs was increasingly distracting now. She sprung onto the steps of the bus, surprised at her own agility. She looked straight down the aisle, and there she saw him. She frowned as he was looking outside the window. She took slow steps, hanging onto the leash overhead to maintain balance on the moving bus, and stood by his side.

She excused herself and moved daintily to the window seat, while he made way for her. She took the same seat despite the fact that there were many seats vacant in the bus. This time, she looked at him for a brief moment, just to keep his image in her mind.

His cologne wafted into her nostrils, and she could also see that he had had a close shave that morning. As the bus trundled on, she felt his hand on her thigh once again and she felt the goose bumps invade her body. His hand had moved much further over her inner thighs and she could not help but to try and push it away as her cheeks turned red. His hands came on stronger as she failed to obstruct his movements in any way. This time, he gripped her inner thigh firmly, the warmth from his hand singed her skin, and she drew a sharp breath.

His hand started to move further up towards her cunt and that is when she whispered at him to stop. His hand touched the seam of her panties just as her heart started to race. Within seconds, he had pulled the seam away, and his fingers were now touching her pussy lips. His face grimaced as he could feel some strain on his hand, and it had to be curled to place the fingers right on the opening of her cunt. His fingers came up against the sticky wetness and he continued rubbing her pussy lips gently.

Mabel just held on to his arm shaking her head in ecstatic agony. Her eyes closed and the morning light lit up her cheeks. She could also feel her nipples perking up through her lacy bra, and her breathing was like someone who was drawing the last breath of their life. Her mind had numbed, and just as she was thinking that this throbbing would never end, Dick stopped and removed his hand from under her skirt.

He removed a handkerchief from his pocket and wiped his hands clean. He rose to go up to the aisle as his destination was drawing close. Only this time he looked at her and smiled, not that Mabel noticed him as she was looking out of the window, trying to distract herself from the recent torment she had to bear.

She was shaking all over, thinking that maybe this was getting out of hand and must stop. Her cheeks were burning, and she could barely keep a smooth rhythm of her breath. She was so lost in thought that she didn't realize the bus was at her stop until the driver called out and woke her from her reverie. She walked quickly towards her home when her elderly neighbor, Mrs. Manson, stopped her on the way. "Oh God" she groaned, since she was looking forward to going home and changing into a fresh pair of panties.

"Mabel, dear, I was meaning to ask you for a favor," she had started to say. "There is a book by a French novelist Pierre Loti, Mon Frère Yves, which I want to read," she had said. Mabel just nodded at her and rushed past her towards her house.

Once in, she threw her purse on the chair, went into the bathroom, and stripped herself naked. She had never really spent a lot of time looking at herself in the mirror, but that evening, she paused and looked at herself in the full-length mirror. She felt her breasts and held them, sensing their enormity in her hands. The softness gave her pleasure and sent throbbing pulses to her pussy. She felt devoured and was beginning to enjoy the sensation. Her hand crept to her pussy, and she began to run her fingers over the lips just as a moan escaped her lips.

She became a bit excited because she had never enjoyed her true sexuality, thanks to her upbringing. She began to rub her lips vigorously and within moments felt an eruption which not only had her breathless, but she was shaking too. She had never experienced this before and was euphoric. In her thoughts, she thanked her fellow bus traveler, and from that day on, her life changed from being a boring bookworm to a desirous lady.

She quickly put on her pajamas and went to have a word with her mother. Her mother had dozed off in her easy chair and a book lay open on her lap. Mabel took the book, placed it on the table, and gently woke up her mother for dinner.

At the dinner table, Mabel spoke about her routine at work and also mentioned her meeting Mrs. Manson. "Since when did she take up to reading? And a French book at that," she chuckled.

During her visits to church on Sundays, Mrs. Mason would usually be sitting next to her. She would regale her with gossip on their walk back home. In bed now, Mabel's thoughts wandered off to her fellow traveler. She did not even know his name, but she felt some connection with him. Should she ask him his name? Oh no, I could not do that, she thought. But she must learn a bit more about him if she wanted to fully enjoy her new found indulgence.

She had not realized that her hand had travelled to her mound. Her fingers played with her pubic hair, and she started to feel a bit uncomfortable. She promised herself to get a razor and shave off her pubic hair the very next day. Having decided that she would make a fresh start, she drifted off to sleep.

When Mabel's alarm went off, she woke up and hurriedly went about her morning routine without giving much thought to what she had planned for the day. When she was in her shower and rubbing the suds off her body, her hand felt her pubic hair and that is when she panicked a bit. She didn't want to dare go on the bus with her pussy in that state. She decided to take a later bus instead of her normal one.

The very first thing she would do is buy an expensive razor. She left home at the usual time and waited at a good vantage point so she could see the inside of the bus. Just then the bus appeared from a distance, and as it neared the stop, she could see "her man" sitting on his usual seat. She could also see him peering out, looking for her, and that is when she felt a sweet warmth in her heart. Once the bus left and was heading on its way, she walked slowly towards the bus stop, humming a tune under her breath.

The sky had a different orange hue, and it was almost cloudless. Mabel had a reason to be happy now. That afternoon during her break, she walked into the nearest store and purchased a razor and some shaving gel. Walking through the aisle towards the cashier, she passed the women's lingerie section and stopped to take a look. One after the other, she went through the rows of panties and then saw something that caught her eye.

This piece was lacy, an off-white color, and it had a slit in the front. She asked the saleswoman to pack 3 of them in various colors. Happy at what she had achieved, she went about her job at the bookstore smiling at her customers and even at her colleagues. That night, she went to bed a bit early and was up much before her alarm went off. She was at the bus stop well in time and boarded the bus when it arrived, smiling to herself.

From the corner of her eye, she could see Mr. Course Hands and her heart swelled up. As usual, she walked to the seat and waited while the man made way for her to move in. As soon as she sat, his hand raised her skirt right to the end of her thighs, as if in a hurry, and immediately found his object of interest.

His fingers tapped lightly, and Mabel could feel the delight in the act as her pussy was now void of hair, and he had a comfortable clearing to touch her slit. She rubbed his arm in encouragement as Dick smiled in earnest. It seemed they both had found each other. The smooth skin enhanced the feel of the whole experience now, so Dick ventured further in while Mabel adjusted her seating so that Dick was able to reach deeper inside her pussy.

As he reached deeper, she felt a sharp pain inside and felt something more oozing out. Dick quickly withdrew his fingers and looked at them, they were bloody and he panicked. "Are you a virgin?" he asked.

Mabel nodded nervously. "Oh damn," he grimaced. Mabel felt a bit guilty but remained quiet. After wiping his hands with his handkerchief, he held out his right hand to Mabel and said "I am Dick, Dick Smith, and I live just a couple of blocks away."

"I am Mabel Swanson and I live nearby too," she said almost breathlessly. Dick had not let go of her hand and she didn't mind. After all, they had just spoken for the first time after all these days. It was a bit weird, but at least there was conversation. Dick spoke about his past in the army and how shrapnel had ruptured his spleen. He was operated on and was given a medical discharge from the Army.

His wife had deserted him and had left their home to explore her dreams in New York theatre. She had sent him the divorce papers after he had learnt that she was living with her stage director. Mabel was awestruck with what she had heard and patted his arm in a comforting way.

Mabel briefly told him about her life, and by the time she had completed, Dick's stop had come up.

He assured her that they would meet as usual, making Mabel's day. Her work day went well. She slipped away for a few moments to go and wash off her soiled panties in the store's restroom. She had quite cleverly set her panties to dry on a hidden ledge so no one could see. Throughout the day, she felt odd being without panties. She was lucky that none of her customers had asked her for a book high up that would have required her to climb on the ladder. She giggled at the naughty thought. She felt good with her drab life going through a whole new different dimension.

What Mabel had come to realize that day was that Dick had been lonely after his wife's departure, and she felt sympathetic towards him. She believed that it was justification for his behavior on the bus. She appreciated his being able to stem what could have been a disastrous situation by breaking into a friendly conversation. She had quite liked that and was now eager to meet him in better environments, rather than a shaky bus.

She started to pay more attention to her appearance, and managed to pick up a few cosmetics that day.

Her rendezvous with Dick were very pleasant, and they greeted each other with a warm hug and he whispered into her ear how beautiful she was. During the course of their conversation, Dick invited her over to his place for dinner that evening. Mabel hesitated at first, but then agreed, provided he would drop her back at her house. Dick smiled in agreement saying that he would even pick her up from her house at 7 p.m., and they both seemed quite happy with the outcome of their small talk.

That evening, Mabel asked her boss if she could leave early, and he agreed. She rushed to the bus stop to board the first available bus home. When she got home, she had a quick shower, running the razor over her pubic area carefully, and then again ran her hand to feel it herself. She felt good and smiled at herself as she knew what was to come that evening. She explained to her mother that she would be having dinner at a new friend's house and that she should be home a bit late. Since the next day was Saturday, there was no reason to worry.

Mabel was waiting on her porch by 6:45 p.m. and exactly at 7, she saw the lone figure of Dick walking at a steady pace towards her house. He waved at her once he saw her. Mabel pranced down her steps to meet him, and they briefly hugged. On the way to his house, he told her that since he lived alone, he hardly found time to clean up the house but he had tried his best. He also confessed to her that he had never done anything like this before and that he had found her to be very attractive and shy. He had gotten carried away in the bus just because of her shyness.

Mabel made a mental note of all what he was saying, but her mind remained in one place: between her legs. She had felt spurred the moment she had set her eyes on him that evening and her entire body had been tingling in anticipation. "I shall not do anything stupid to spoil the evening," she had said to herself.

Just as Dick bent over to open his door with his keys, Mabel caught herself looking at his tight ass and wondered how it would feel in her hands. Her soft giggle made Dick turn around and ask if anything was the matter.

"Oh nothing," said Mabel, embarrassed now as she entered the door. He followed her in as she stood close by nervously taking in the simple interior. Dick came up close to her and held her waist bringing her body close to his. Mabel hesitatingly put her hands on his shoulders and that is when he bent over to kiss her lips. She had never been kissed before, and so her initial reaction was dread, but in an instant, she began to suck at his lips driving her state to a different level.

Her eyes closed as she began to relish the intimacy. Dick had pushed his crotch between her legs, and her body was against the wall. His hands rushed to her breasts and he began to massage them as he felt the softness through the thin fabric of her bra and dress. His hands were doing wonders to her body as she felt the tingling between her legs grow more intense. She was a bit breathless and began to gasp. Dick stopped and asked if she was alright. Mabel smiled and nodded, too shy to acknowledge that she was really enjoying herself.

She had never imagined it to be so good. She slipped one of her hands towards Dick's crotch and felt his engorged penis through his denim, and she gasped more from her discovery and delight than fright. She did not wait for Dick to say anything, immediately kneeled in front of him, unzipped his pants hurriedly, and pulled down the pants as well his underpants. Her nostrils were hit by a strong odor emitting from his cock. It was something wild, but she found it gripping as she ran her hand up and down the length of his manhood taking her time to look at it closely as her fascination began to rise at fervently.

She kissed the tip nervously, not really knowing what it would feel and then hesitantly covered it with her mouth. Her tongue ran on the head over and over again sending ripples of pleasure to Dick's body. He groaned aloud and Mabel stopped, looking up at his face. He looked down at her face and smiled encouragingly. He pulled away her pins from her hair and gently ran his fingers through it. Taking it as a cue, she began to suck his cock, drawing out some pre-cum. She gulped it without any problem and continued to bob her head over Dick's hardness.

Dick stopped her midway and asked her to rise up. He shook off his pants and underwear and walked towards a chair, holding her hand. Mabel followed, wondering if she had done well or not. He pulled down her panties and pulled her dress over her head leaving her completely naked, except for her bra. She felt completely exposed, but pride took over as she realized that her pussy looked good without any hair.

She coolly reached behind her back and

undid her bra just as Dick stood before her unbuttoning his shirt and admiring her body. His eyes grew wider when he saw her perfectly rounded breasts. He grasped them intensely and began to suck them eagerly and buckled down in a kneeling position.

Mabel held his head and steadied him and felt pushed into the chair. Now, he had his hands around her buttocks, which felt soft in his hands. He played his tongue on her nipples one after the other, but Mabel was lost in her own world. She was going through one of the best experiences of her life. She held his head close to her breasts and the smile never left her face.

Within a few moments, Dick shifted and moved his mouth away from her breasts, kissing her torso and navel. He then surprised her by lifting her legs over his shoulders. He sank his mouth straight to her pussy and just as he did that Mabel just opened her mouth, her eyes wide and she let out a sigh, feeling a different kind of pleasure emitting from her cunt. She felt as if she was slipping into a deep crevasse as she experienced her very first sensation against her clitoris.

She moaned aloud, and her breathing became uneven. She was gasping for breath and felt completely vulnerable. Dick seemed quite experienced in such matters as he flicked his tongue in an attempt to tickle Mabel's clitoris. Dick did not realize that he was giving this woman so much pleasure, but he did feel his own adrenaline shoot up. Mabel had clasped her legs together not realizing that Dick's head was in between them. She was shuddering, and the first wave of her orgasm hit her intensely.

She had gone wild in the chair flailing her hands and moving her head from side to side. Dick held her steady as she started to sob and yet again she raised her waist high, this time surprising Dick with her vigor. She calmed down after a while, her eyes closed, and she murmured "that was just beautiful, oh my God, it was heavenly," in between her heavy breathing. Dick smiled and wiped his mouth. He kissed her lightly on her lips, and this time Mabel held him close with her arms entwined around his head.

"Oh my darling, you are so sweet," she said listlessly as if she had tired herself after climbing up a mountain.

Dick held her head between his hands and replied, "I am glad you enjoyed it."

He picked her up and took her to his bedroom, where he laid her down. Mabel felt relaxed and cozy on the bed with fresh sheets. Her eyes were now mischievous as she struck an erotic pose for Dick with one hand over her pussy and the other rubbing her nipple, biting her lower lip.

Dick scooped Mabel back in his arms as he positioned himself between her legs. He kissed her breasts, and she began to run her hands over his back, grazing it with her fingernails. She was about to give herself to a stranger she had just met a few days back. She knew it, and strangely enough, it did not bother her a bit. Meanwhile, Dick excused himself and went into the bathroom only to return with a tube of petroleum jelly. He brought a small dollop and applied it generously over his rock hard penis even as Mabel stretched out to help, but her assistance was gracefully declined.

Once he thought he was ready, he brought his cock over, rubbing it on her now wet pussy. Then with some jerky motions, he pushed it inside. Mabel's eyes shut tight that very instant as she felt a jabbing pain in her pussy and she let out a yelp. Dick stopped inserting his cock midway and drew it out. Mabel gestured to him to continue and once again he pushed it inside. This time, he did not feel any obstruction, but he felt the tightness of Mabel's velvety hole.

He stroked his cock very slowly so as to not cause any further pain. After making certain that he wasn't hurting her, he got into a rhythmic motion. Mabel felt her pussy being ravaged slowly and steadily. It was not too long before Dick began to move at a faster pace and it seemed like Mabel was able to take him in well and also start enjoying the sensation, albeit with a little bit of pain.

Dick brought his hands over her breasts and massaged them with delight, and this also heightened their pleasures. Soon enough, he had started to feel his blood rising to the head of his penis, and within seconds, he withdrew his cock and sprayed Mabel's stomach with his thick and rich cream. He collapsed over Mabel's body, inert and breathing heavily, while she stroked his hair so as to calm him down.

She kissed his head a few times when Dick looked up and said "I think I love you." These words were manna from the heavens for Mabel as she hugged Dick to her chest and she responded with glee: "I love you too, darling."

8 ACHES OF LUST

Andria White was born in Colorado to parents that ran a successful adventure sports business. As she grew up, Andria could usually be found at the desk assisting her parents after school. Most of their visitors were pretty impressed by the information the perky eight year old would throw at them, especially when it came to white-water rafting, kayaking, cycling, rock climbing, and horseback riding.

Her first experience with her sexuality had taken place in quite a rather common manner. She had been in the shower, and when she had placed the shower head close to her tender pussy, hot sensations had exploded from her there, frightening and exciting her all at once. That had led her to try out other experiences, and while away at college, she had several flings with the young men there, but none ever made her really feel the way she could make herself feel. After college, she headed off for New York City and the hostel that was all she could afford her first few months in the city.

She got off the bus and walked the blocks between the hostel and the Port Authority station, drinking in the sights of the city. Once at the hostel, she went into her small, seedy room and tossed her bags down, too eager to sit still. She knew that she had to find a job before her savings were gone. She took a quick shower, changed into some comfortable clothes, and went to the reception. As she was inquiring for a newspaper, she caught sight of an Asian man looking at her.

The woman at the desk introduced them by saying, "Mr. Han, this is Andria from Colorado, and she could use a job. Andria, Mr. Han runs a travel agency, and he often stops by here to put his cards and brochures in our city attractions box."

Mr. Han handed Andria his card and asked her to be at the address by 9 a.m. the next day. L&L Travel Enterprise was the name of the company and Andria quickly learned the ropes.

One night, Mr. Han called her into his office. "Adlia," he said (for some quaint reason, he could not pronounce her name cleanly, always it with an L instead of the R). "Mr Chi and his wife here would like to visit your home state, Cololado. Can you help them?" he asked.

"Of course Mr Han, with pleasure," she responded enthusiastically.

Mr. Han excused himself to go to the washroom as Andria began to rattle off the scopes of adventure in her home state. In her enthusiastic babble, she had leaned on Mr. Han's desk and her buttocks looked very enticing to anyone entering the office. Mr. Han entered the office, and he froze as he stared at what caught his attention. He could not help but reach out to his crotch, trying to hide the hardness which was rising to obvious proportions. He returned to his seat and pretended to be interested in what Andria was telling his clients. Soon, to his utter relief, they left.

He rose and surprised himself by laying his hand on Andria's thigh. Without a word, he came close to her. Andria felt taken aback for a moment but soon realized why she was not objecting to her boss's daring endeavor. His hand felt good on her thighs even through the stockings she had worn. She felt a raw hunger in her groin. It had such a long time since she had been fucked, and she was enamored by this short yet well-built man. She spread her legs and rolled down her sheer panties.

Without a word, Han knelt and inhaled deeply, taking in the smell of sheer femininity at its submissive, yet wild, best. Andria had always been hygienic, and her clean-shaven pussy looked radiant gleaming at the dim lights which illuminated the room. Her wetness was very obvious as some juice dripped below on the carpet. She was breathing heavily as Han expertly licked and sucked at her velvety cunt. She began to run her hand through his jet black hair, encouraging him to do his best. Han's tongue danced all over her pink vaginal opening making her sigh every other second. He performed this task like an expert, dipping and stretching it gently with his tongue. His hands moved to her breasts squeezing them gently at first and then harder.

Andria was so excited that she unzipped her skirt and pulled down her bra, giving Han her beautiful well-rounded breasts. She had never felt like this before, sluttish and brutally hungry for being felt. The feeling began to peak slowly within her as Han stood up and opened his pants and let them flop on the floor. His boxers came off next exposing a hard an evenly measured cock, red and stiff.

Andria took one look at it and went down on her knees, closing her mouth over the knobby head. Han gasped and closed his hands on her hair, forming a tight fist, tugging the silken hair roughly. Andria took his cock deep inside her mouth, then bring it out and then give friendly nibbles to the rim as well as the head, hoisting Han's pleasure to immeasurable heights.

Finally, he pulled his cock away from her mouth leaving her gasping in surprise as some pre-cum dribbled on her chin. She looked up innocently like a little girl who had been deprived of her favorite lollipop.

He looked down upon her. Her eyes were wide with surprise and her lower lip was being bruised by his teeth. He pushed her down gently on the table. He spread her legs and brought his hard cock to her pussy lips straying it a bit on the lips itself. Andria's eyes were shut, and she struggled to move her moist cunt closer to the cock. Han pushed his knobby cock hard into her moist softness. The knobby head took some effort to be pushed inside, but once it was, Han felt the walls of the vulva enclose his manhood warmly. And just then, the first wave of an orgasm hit Andria as she stifled a scream with a whispered yes. It was a hiss more than her voice. But that did not stop Han from his activity. He moved with an even motion, firm and almost with discipline. Each stroke renewed her pleasure, and she felt her pussy wanting to take in the whole cock of this man. His movements began to gather speed. She raised herself to meet him midway so as to help him take her generously. He withdrew from her pussy as Andria orgasmed. Han's cock spewed all over her flat stomach, as she screamed with joy and sobbed uncontrollably. Her whole body shook as the effects of the torrential orgasm rushed through her. Han simply plopped over her body, kissing her softly and whispering endearment.

Ten Years Later

Andria had to take over the agency when, Han, on one of his numerous trips to China, succumbed to a massive heart attack while on a flight. Han's wife was only too happy to surrender the reigns of the agency to Andria as she had always stayed away from his business. She had preferred to be a homebody and would often prod Han to return to China. As luck would have it, she was accompanying Han on this trip to attend a nephew's wedding when tragedy had struck.

Andria had worked really hard and earned a name in the industry, not only in America but also in Europe as well as Asia. L&L Travel Enterprise had moved to a higher rung in the travel and lifestyle ladder. Their services were the most sought by many.

The agency was known to offer luxury tours to affluent gentry. One of their most favored offerings was the Privy Tours. A Bentley would arrive at the client's residence and whisk them away to a private Airstrip where a sleek Gulfstream IV super-luxurious aircraft would be waiting for them to fly off to an island destination in the Far East. The client couple would be pampered with exclusive services while on their way. The biggest surprise would be that they would find themselves completely alone, barring the three or four member staff who would be manning the luxury holiday destination. Each trip was memorable for clients. L&L Travel's well-oiled staff numbered high, ensuring that the clients did not have any problems and all was smooth.

Andria had learned of a remote island in the Pacific region which was practically without any human habitation. It had a natural waterfall and rich flora and fauna. Even the weather was mostly stable. The island was within the territory of a local tribesman called Sula. The head of the tribe was a suave, 40-year-old Harvard graduate named Marico. His name was acquired along with his other habits, mostly influenced by the Western culture. He ruled over a band of 1,200 families spread over 30-odd islands of the Pacific. The Kure Atoll and the Pearl and Hermes Atoll lay 125 miles to the west and 115 miles to the east, respectively. There were uninhabited coral formations in the vicinity. The US government had set aside taking over the islands with an understanding that they would be allowed to set up as and when they would want. If L&L was to get exclusive rights over the island Ro, as it was called, it would not only fetch a premium price for visitations bringing in enough cash but it would also become one of the agencies a prime opulent venture.

Andria knew that the key to this deal was the consent of the honorable king Marico. She asked her PA to book her on a flight to Hawaii from where she could take a boat ride to Maramba, the capital island and the seat of power. She had no idea of what or how she was going to do to get this to happen but her mind was made up.

She packed carefully, making sure that she had the right kind of clothes and accessories for the trip. She cut her hair short, and this had her stand out from the crowd. Her new look had a faint resemblance to that of Halle Berry.

Her flight to Hawaii was without any problems, and she proceeded to the travel lounge nodding and waving to acquaintances she had made over the years in the island city. Perching herself on the bar stool, she ordered for a "Bikini Martini" to get into the spirit although it was early for her. She looked around at the cool interiors, studying the other occupants of the lounge bar. She did not notice a tall man take the chair next to hers. Dressed in a stark white linen slacks and a jacket and a soothing mauve-colored shirt made out of organic cotton, he had already drawn eyeballs upon his entry, but since Andria had been looking at the far side to her left, she missed this mystery man.

"A Cranberry Sea Breeze please," a baritone voice rang out. It was so sharp that it made Andria turn around in an instant almost embarrassing herself she smiled. His face was an instant attraction. It could make even a "Granny" blush with pleasure. "Are you on a holiday?" he asked breaking the ice.

Normally, Andria would not talk to strangers, but this hulk was an exception. "I am here on a business trip," she responded, breathless.

He asked if she was in the travel

business, and on her response, he offered his time to her. "Oh no, I am fine as my business here is a bit confidential," she burst out but regretted it as it sounded sinister. Foolishly enough, she blurted out her purpose, and it was then that the stranger stuck out his hand. Surprised, Andria responded by giving her hand.

"Marico, but you may call me Mario," he said. "I am impressed by your efforts, and I think we should immediately proceed to Ro."

Dumbstruck, yet pleased by her luck, she followed him like a lamb, baggage in tow.

They had boarded a custom-built super-luxury yacht which was berthed at the pier. The thrumming of the twin-powered boat sent faint vibrations to Andria's pussy, and she nearly stumbled. Thankfully, nobody noticed as Mario barked orders to his crew and within minutes they were off. Somehow, Mario had a magical effect on Andria as she sprawled on the deck settee on receiving encouragement from him.

She did not realize that her two top buttons of her blouse had given way, letting out one of her red lace clad breasts for him to see. Mario had been looking away and was telling her about the conditions at the island. So mesmerized was she that she did not make any move to button up her blouse.

When Mario looked in her direction, it was his turn to be captivated. She was petite, yet the proportion of her breasts and her buttocks gave her the unique sense of attractiveness that his loins seemed to get embarrassingly restless. Growing bold, Mario effortlessly raised her body in his arms before carrying her below into the cool serenity of the VIP stateroom and gently propping her on the king-sized bed.

Andria did nothing but stare at Mario's handsome face, she had completely forgotten her mission. Her only focus was the "magnetic" Mario, her host for now.

Mario had stripped himself of his clothes and was now bare bodied, clothed only by his "banana hammock." She turned and reached out to hold his massive rock-hard cock. She drew herself closer and sucked hungrily. Her intermittent "sexcapades" with Han were wonderful while they lasted, and during that time, she had become addicted to daring sex and longed to taste the cock of the man in front of her. She reached out to hold the massive rod of pleasure. Her head bobbed, famished mouth sending waves of scintillating pleasure to Mario's head. She began to shiver at the prospect of having her tight hole filled with that heated length. Her nipples began to give her painful pleasures, and she was lost in her trance when Mario held her hair in his hands and pulled her off his penis and pushed her on the bed.

Kneeling, he put his mouth on Andria's throbbing pussy. She welcomed the touch and spread her legs wide open. Her clit was throbbing in anticipation of the big moment to come. Mario licked her cunt lips with passion and in an earnest desire to give her the pleasure. Just as his tongue touched her clitoris, it swelled and she began to gasp in pleasure. It was something she had never felt or even expected. Mario had done wonders with his tongue as no man had done before this. She came hard, and suddenly, her legs jerking as she groaned and held his head closer to her pussy. She could not stop shuddering, but finally she collapsed on her back.

Not expecting anything, Andria allowed him to take the lead. Then with a swift and supple motion, he held her waist and raised her to his chest. Andria's eyes widened in surprise and dread, but that quickly settled as he asked her to guide his rod into her pussy while she was suspended in his grip. Once her pussy lips came in contact with his cock, he lowered her slowly, holding her waist firmly yet gently. Andria felt her cunt engorge the thickness of his manhood and felt a bit of pain as her tissue seemed to stretch a bit. But in the next few moments, she had managed to swallow it within her hot, juicy honey pot. Mario began to lift her and drop her in slow deliberate motions, both to enhance his pleasure as well as hers. Andria held his neck interlocking her fingers around it. She took the cue and began to "ride" Mario's cock matching his motions. She could not help moaning in pleasure and did it shamelessly, not even bothering to keep it low. The yacht would roll intermittently as it would meet waves at sea. But it did not bother them.

Mario's strokes became more ferocious as he too began to moan loudly. He held her buttocks while pushing her deeper into the mattress with his weight. Cupping each in his massive hands, he squeezed them in unison, sending a different kind of pleasure through her body. She was getting a feel of how it would be if her "other hole" was to be penetrated.

Mario pulled out of Andria's quivering cunt so his fountain of semen splattered over her buttocks, some of it dripped down her ass crack. He leaned heavily on her and the wall supporting both of them. He kissed her lips, and she hungrily took his tongue into her mouth. Finally, she laid her head on his shoulder, as a sense of calming and secure feeling enveloped her. Mario gently moved her to the bed and put her down. He excused himself and went to the washroom. Andria looked outside through the porthole and saw some birds. Her heart was already flying and her body was tingling after her tryst with the king. What was she supposed to do now? Say thank you your highness? She closed her eyes and smiled. It seemed like a sure bet that she had won the bid to use his island for her company.

Needless to say, she had managed to strike a deal with King Marico, besides earning a place on his bed whenever she visited her most successful acquisition.

9 A MUSE FOR USE AND DELIGHTS

It had been raining the whole week and the weather was going to be even rougher during the next few days as was being said by the television newscaster. Laura stretched lazily; eyes still shut and reached out to touch the bedstead and woke up with a start. Her hand had come up against a metal one, brass to be exact, instead of the wooden one which was on her bed.

She sat up and tried to recall her previous night and dull ache started to knock her temples. She looked further towards the French windows and was greeted by the faint San Francisco skyline, hiding behind the mist which hovered over the city. She was still fuzzy when it hit her. She had spent her night with Chef Durante and the fact that she was naked she was sure that she had even fucked with him.

Oh no! she thought and holding her head between her hands, she wracked her brains to bring some sense to what had happened. Her heart skipped a beat when she did not find him anywhere in the house. Then her attention was drawn to a note on the table. "Sleep as much as you want but don't be late for work. There is cab fare on the bedside table for you to get home and back to work,"the note said. Laura ran to the bathroom for a shower, hoping that it could help clear her head.

She had drunk some tequila at the restaurant just before leaving for home at the end of the day and was caught up in the street with no cabs, as torrential rains drummed the streets without any letting up. She knew that she shouldn't have had more than two shots, but she had been egged on by the French sous chef, Pierre, to have more. Hence she got carried away and went ahead only to regret much later as she stood at the curb, just outside the service entrance, waiting for a cab ride home, drenched to her skin. Suddenly sports sedan had screeched to a halt right in front of her and the door had opened. She had peeped inside and could barely make out a large figure of Chef Durante.

Relieved, she had smiled and gotten inside and felt his hand patting her thigh as s sign of reassurance. She remembered telling him that she stayed quite far towards Oakland just before the bridge. She also recalled him asking her to spend the night at his place. She had nodded coyly considering it being quite late, as it was almost 2 a.m. During the journey, he was quiet and Laura had kept her chatter on in an attempt to catch his attention.

Arnaud Durante was a large framed Frenchman; celebrated for his tongue tickling culinary expertise had earned him "King Chef" in the industry. Executive Chef, C.E.C., and Food and Beverage Director at the Westin St. Francis, he had earned his name after having enchanted the likes of former US President Jimmy Carter and his 1,200 guests, the Dalai Lama, including the numerous Hollywood celebrities. He lived alone and preferred the company of his well-behaved Labrador, Minsk.

Laura had already made friends with Minsk when friendly canine would visit the hotel's kitchen on occasions. Minsk had recognized Laura and had run to her side wagging his tail. It was a big penthouse, overlooking the bay area on the one side and the Zigzag Street on the other. There was a sundeck, up ahead adjoining the living room. Arnaud had gone to his room and returned with a white robe which would reach her knees. "Go and get out of those wet clothes," he had said in a soft, yet stern voice, as he would back at the hotel. Laura had done as she was told but she had still felt a bit groggy.

As she had stepped out, Arnaud had stood perplexed, looking at her medium sized frame, as her breasts stood out, slightly over proportioned to the rest of her body. He had inquired if she wanted a drink and had gone behind the bar to get one, for himself. Laura had settled for a glass of Bordeaux and raised her glass towards the chef's direction.

Taking a sip she had relished the wine inside her mouth before swallowing it. She had not realized that Arnaud had come close to her and only became aware when he laid his hand on her shoulder. She had looked up at him and set her glass on the low table by the leather sofa. She kneeled in front of him, unzipped his trouser and seeking his cock, had brought it out. It had looked quite smallish in size as she had begun to massage it in her hands using them expertly, when within no time she could feel it harden and grow in size. She had kissed the head of the cock once and then had licked the length of it, stopping for a while to suck at his genitals. Arnaud had not looked down at all but had his eyes shut, wondering If he was doing anything wrong, but it did bring him some relief after a tough day at work.

Even as Laura had begun to use her mouth on his genitals her hands were busy stroking the length of his penis. Her cunt was already draining itself with juices, firing up the heat in the pit of her stomach. She was groggy, but that did not matter as she was indulging in her one of her favorite passions. She was breathing hard and her nostrils flared having had to use her mouth to do the talking. She brought her attention back to Arnaud's, now erect penis, and her eyes had sparkled as she got to see what magic her skill had produced. Just the thought of Arnaud's cock in her mouth was driving her up the wall as she had begun to suck it with aggression.

She had not wanted him to change his mind and had begun to secretly fantasize as to how he would fuck her on one of the kitchen tables, or maybe in his palatial office, or even in his car parked in the basement. Her thoughts seemed to have produced even more sensuality as her head had started to bob up and down in fierce rapidity.

One of her hands had crept over his buttocks and the nails had begun to dig in slightly as the other hand had held her genitals as also keeping some pressure on the area just behind his balls. This had a telling effect on Arnaud as he moaned loudly and kept saying "Foutre", or fuck in French. He had held her head with both his hands and moved it faster so that she could bring him his release. A few minutes later, hot white semen burst out of his cock. Arnaud had held her head in place spraying her face with the mushy fluid. Some drops had even escaped over her head on her hair.

Arnaud then picked up Laura and kissed her face and lips. He had reamed her lips with his own and had pushed his tongue deeper into her mouth while his hands had felt her breasts from under the open robe which had come open now. He toyed with her breasts likening it to how he would examine fruits in his restaurant kitchen. Laura had found herself in heaven to be toyed like that by her superior, whom she adored for his gastronomic proficiency. The next instance she could recall was when they were both in bed and Arnaud had turned her over so that her well rounded buttocks were seen. He ran his fingers through the crack of her ass and took it as far as the pussy, which had her draw breath sharply.

He had then entered her cunt and pounded it over and over as she managed to take it all in even as she gritted her teeth and began to mouth words like

"Fuck me, fuck me harder, oh lord please fuck me." This had made Arnaud drive in more powerfully as he stood with one leg on the bed and the other steady on the floor.

Laura had started to feel her orgasm giving her spasms and she shuddered as he came hard. She had even stifled her scream and let out her breath only after Arnaud had pulled out of her yet again spraying his cum on her back. He had then excused himself and gone into the bathroom. Laura had followed him and once again the couple regaled themselves under the hot showers of water as then beat over their bodies. Later after having dried themselves, they had laid on the bed and drifted off to sleep.

Laura was happy by the end of the day as she arrived at work in good time and then received some envious stares from her colleagues when Chef Durante had called for her. She had been instructed to make a separate set of sauces for that evening's dinner ensemble. The chef's decision was not totally unfounded as Laura had this mysterious sense of taste and smell, she could create a masterpiece cuisine within minutes and this had the approval of not only her superiors but also the restaurant managers and owners. She was even allowed to try out her own dishes and with some guidance from the sous chefs, she often succeeded in winning accolades for the restaurant and for herself from the diners. Besides her passion for sex, her only other major interest was cooking.

Her interest in sex had ignited when she had returned early from her college, The California Culinary Academy, to find her cousin sister Maureen in bed naked, masturbating to her heart's content. She had watched keenly from behind the door of the room which both shared. Maureen was using her fingers proficiently and it could be seen that what she was doing was having an electric like effect even on Laura. That evening when both of them were alone in the room, she had teased her cousin about what she had seen that late afternoon. Her cousin had later convinced her to try it herself by even sucking her pussy.

The result was that Laura got into the habit of masturbation or if she was invited by any man, she would have sex. It was like non-liquid remedy which would give her agility in her daily life. Until the time she was in college, she kept restraint on her sexual escapades but indulged in masturbation in the privacy of her room.

Her college had sent her to the Westin St Francis for her internship and during the interview she had impressed the panelists with her in depth knowledge of spices and their flavors. On her first day at the hotel, she was asked by her supervisor to help out another intern, an Italian boy who spoke little English but with a quaint accent. "They tell me that you good coo,k" he asked with his weird pronunciation, "but are also good fuck?" he added. He also praised her breasts no end as her tits seemed to burst out of her uniform and some of could be seen through shirt buttons.

"Come, we go to store room to find out," he said. Laura was petrified at such a direct approach. She refused to relent outright and stomped out of the room, angry at the other interns remarks, and just as she was going to move out at the door, her supervisor intervened and told her that she had to go to the storeroom to do an inventory check on all that was kept in there. He told her Lucian, the Italian boy, was familiar with the process and she will not have any difficulty. It was only then that she realized that Lucian had played a prank on her and laughed.

However during the break, she asked him about his experience in sex and was taken aback as he responded quite positively, without batting an eyelid. "We

Italians get hot blood, and so natural lovers. I know you not believe, but I show you and then you happy," he interjected. Lucian had arrived in the US just three years before as an immigrant. His father was already a citizen of the country. He had sought cookery as his professional option since he loved to cook, thanks to his mother's love for cooking. "My mother cook for big dinners with 100 guests," he boasted. That evening he invited her over to his house for dinner and Laura, happily, relented.

That evening was when Laura discovered her limit of sexual fervor when Lucian took her in his arms and swung her into the house, when she had rung the bell. She was dressed in a shirt and jeans with two buttons open, which was not to expose her cleavage but because the buttons could not hold shut. Now this did not miss Lucian's eyes as the very first thing he did after the welcoming waltz was plant his lips on the her bursting, voluptuous breasts. So enamored was he, that he began to lick the crevasse between her peaks of pleasure. His licking was so sensual that it sent ripples of pleasure all over Laura's body that she could feel some trickle of fresh cunt juice as her eyes just closed relishing the sensation. As he continued to use his tongue like a veteran, he used his hands to unbutton her shirt and bring out both the breast out of the thin lacy bra that she had worn for the occasion. Laura held his head as his tongue, lips and teeth worked feverishly all over her breasts, with reverence to his attention. He sucked on her nipples covering her areola with his mouth while he used his tongue to tickle her nipples which sent a fresh wave up her spine.

He also used his hands to massage the other breast daintily and this enhanced her pleasure even more. A fresh stream of cunt fluid began to trickle through her wafer thin panties and settled at the edge of her crotch, even showing the dampness. Meanwhile, Lucian took off her belt and pulled down her jeans and he was about to tear off her panties when Laura stopped him pleading him to be patient. She stepped away and undressed with such grace that Lucian let out an eager growl. Sensing his urgency, she also took time to undress him like a dutiful lover and gasped at the sight at the size of his engorged penis. She was raving mad as she knew that she was about to have one of the most beautiful erotic experiences of her life. She cradled it in her soft hands and used her long fingernails to run it over his erection. Lucian stood proudly as Laura took her time to examine his masterpiece. She was highly impressed by this Italian youth and seemed eager to take this to the next level. Laura had learnt the ropes of sucking cock by using her dildos and she had proficient help from Maureen, who had claimed that she was the best cock sucker in the neighborhood. She had pulled back his foreskin and used her tongue to wet the top of the head.

There was some pre-cum which had suddenly appeared on the head, which Laura quickly wiped with her tongue. Lucian held her hair in a fist and tugged it a few times, which felt great and Laura's mouth covered the cock. She also used her nail in scratching at his genitals and this gentle scraping gave Lucian immense pleasure.

They both seemed to be complimenting each other bodies and they were beginning their ascent to the next level. Lucian realized that he was being selfish so he pulled out his cock from Laura's mouth surprising her by what he had done. There was an old wooden easy chair in the corner of the room. This chair had a unique hand rest as it extended out so the person sitting could raise his or her feet and bring it to rest over the extended arm. Lucian guided Laura to the chair and made her sit down. He had then raised her legs to bring it on the extended arm rest. This way he had an easy access to her wet cunt as her legs had to be spread wide open.

Without wasting too much time, he sank his mouth in her pussy lips and began to feast on her labia and suddenly Laura felt that she had been lifted into a different dimension. Lucian seemed to be a connoisseur of the woman's anatomy and it showed in his enthusiasm as well as the delight on Laura's face. His tongue darted in and out of her dripping cunt and Laura saw the difference in her indulgence now. It was true as Lucian made her feel complete and she savored the experience.

Lucian had found her clitoris and he began to suck it in his mouth with a vigor new for her. She felt a faint tugging at the pit of her stomach and the sensation began to grow more intense. Suddenly she began to spasm wildly and she let out a shriek but her voice sounded different. Just then her pussy began to flood and jets of fluid squirted out onto Lucian's face and he moved away and laughed.

This had been her first intense orgasm and she would never forget it. After a while he helped her up as she had requested to use the washroom. Inside, she looked at her face as there was a faint glow in her cheeks and she just could not get rid of that smile on her face. Soon she returned to see Lucian holding out a glass of wine which she readily accepted. No words were exchanged as both of them were beaming at each other while admiring each other's bodies.

Laura could not wait and so she came into Lucian's arms and they kissed, rolling their tongues into each other's mouths. Lucian admitted that he had thoroughly enjoyed doing what he did as Laura's body features were a treat. It was true as her breasts gave her a provocative look, and any male who admired female beauty would not have resisted just staring at her.

After they were done with their drinks, Lucian quickly laid the table and brought out a serving plate of lasagna al forno a simple dish of baked lasagna with two portions of baked fish, a recipe he had picked up from his grandmother. It was obvious for that the meal was just an excuse and both of them finished off their food within no time. Now naked, they shared a cigarette in Lucian's bedroom which was small, yet the ambience was good for some sex. Lucian had not stopped stroking Laura's breasts as he may have thought to make the best of the time and he wanted to keep her sex drive alive. Laura had turned her attention on Lucian's cock and massaged it lovingly, staring at it in open admiration. She knew that she was going to be pleasured by it. It was evident that she had started to like Lucian not just as a colleague but as a lover.

Lucian climbed over her body and stroked her pussy with his cock slowly sliding it inside it. He did feel some obstruction but his persistence paid off and he was able to enter with some jerky motions. Laura did feel some pain at first, being a virgin; she had never experienced sex with any male in the past but her vagina had been plundered by her constant use of her numerous dildos she had with her.

After a few strokes Lucian suggested that they change the positions and he had her turn over and entered her cunt from behind. This way he could also massage her breasts and Laura too enjoyed it not only for the difference but it was an additional experience for her. As his cock grazed her pussy's edges, she felt her orgasm building up and within no time she had her spasms. Lucian was yet to reach his climax and increased his pace and just as he was about to burst, he pulled out spraying her back with his hot cum. Exhausted, they kissed for a while and fell into each other's arms, slipping into deep sleep.

After that this had become a routine for both of them and it became apparent that they were an inseparable couple. Both Lucian and Laura were careful not to exhibit their fondness towards each other when at work but that they were good friends. Their going was good until the time when Lucian's father took up a job in distant New York and Lucian was forced to go along. It broke Laura's heart but she promised to stay in touch and if providence prevails, even join him there.

Things had changed since then until the time Laura spent the night at Chef Durante's house. From then on her new journey had commenced and she did not have to look back. Both her passions had come alive and thereafter there was no wishful thinking.

10 MY WICKED DESIRES

I don't exactly recall as to when I had taken a liking for sex but for me it wasn't just a liking. It was an obsession. However, there is one instance which has remained emblazoned in my mind. It was during my last year in school and everyone had been busy preparing for the prom. Since I was in charge of the decorations, I had spent the night before supervising the preparations in the gym.

The next day I had gone looking for a broom and since it was a Saturday I had gone looking for it in the store room of the school. Inside the storeroom was a bed which the school janitor would rest during breaks. I lay down for a while and did not realize when I fell asleep.

When I woke up it was dark and just as

I got off the bed to leave I saw the door open slowly. Not knowing what to do I thought the best thing that I could do was to hide behind the cupboard. It was the janitor's assistant. I was surprised to see him in school, as it was his day off. Before I could get up and excuse myself to leave he had taken off his overalls and he was naked under them.

The one thing which caught my attention was his enormous cock. It was unlike anything I had ever laid my eyes on. A hot tightness had formed in the pit of my stomach as I mentally started to fondle it in my hands and I had not realized that my hand was inside my short skirt through my panties, playing with my pussy lips. I was very horny then and felt the heat rise up to my throat. Just as I was about to let out a moan, my other hand leapt to my mouth to stifle my voice. The man had seemed to enjoy his freedom as he stroked it slowly for a while. Then he took his jeans and shirt off the hook on the wall and proceeded to don them. Within the next few moments he was gone and I realized that all this may have happened in a flash that I had to pinch my arm to assure myself that what I had seen was real and not a dream. I managed to come out the room, unnoticed and went straight to the gym where the others had been waiting. I was in a daze and hardly paid heed to the complaining girls around me. I remember I had picked up my bag and hurried home without even a word to anyone. At home in bed I lay in bed, stripping myself of my panties after locking my door. I ran my fingers over my pussy lips and found my clitoris. By stroking myself I was able to achieve a good orgasm. I recall I had shut my eyes and fantasized being ravaged by that enormous cock I had seen that evening.

I am Carla Mason and I was raised in Glendale, California. My parents were preachers and I was brought up under a lot of vigil to lead a good life. I did as I was told and even kept away from "bad company" just so that I did not bring any misery to my beloved parents. I prayed like every good child would and did well in school. In other words, I was a good girl during my formative years. I lost my mother to cancer, and within a year, my father passed away from an illness even the doctors could not comprehend. By then this state helped me prepare myself to face the world on my own.

Now, I was away from my small town, having done a course as a chiropractor and I had started practicing in the county hospital. I was ever so diligent in my work and was liked by everyone amongst the staff. I was happy but I was craving a fuck. My bedroom drawer was practically loaded with various kinds of vibrators, beads and even the Burmese Ben WA balls for doing my Kegel exercises. I would insert the balls inside my vagina and then sit on the rocking chair by the window, watching life go by while I rocked myself to some great stimulation. My daily schedule was an easy one since I would be referred to just a handful of patients every other day. Most of the other times, I would ogle at young men visiting the hospital from my vantage point inside the reception counter. From where I sat I could easily lay my eyes on their crotches or their butts.

I loved those moments when I would just fantasize how their cocks would feel inside my pussy and immediately I would begin getting wet. I would quietly slip my hands inside my scrub pants through the elastic band and touch myself at the core of my sexuality, if there was no one around me. I was already aware that at some point I would come out of my shell and be more promiscuous but I did not want to be labeled an easy lay or a whore. Little did I know that I would be soon taking my obsession to a higher level.

One Saturday, which was my day off, I

had gone to the basement of my apartment to use the Laundromat. I was thinking of visiting my new friend that lived a few blocks away. I was lost in thoughts when my crotch accidentally touched the edge of the drier. Just as the machine began to go through its spin dry mode, it began to vibrate and send crazy sensations into my pussy. I was taken by the sudden surge of massive vibrations centering just into my pussy. I was completely wet within moments and I shut my eyes to take the pleasure of this unusual method. As I recall, I was even whimpering like a pup as heave after heave began to assault my cunt. I had been wearing a flimsy pair of shorts made out of linen which I usually wore at home and nothing inside.

So the intensity was even more engaging and it was no wonder I was lifted into a different dimension. I was totally lost in my own whirling universe, pushing my cunt further onto the edge and almost lost my balance, had it not been for a small ledge, used for keeping boxes of detergent powder. I gripped the edge and hung on there as I was hit by a typhoon and I shook like a dry leaf.

The orgasm was heavenly and I was breathless for some time. I collapsed slowly over the machine and actually kissed it twice, as if to say thank you.

Little did I know that all this while a set of eyes had been watching me.

He must have been there much before I had come but I had failed to notice him as he was behind the dividing wall which was about shoulder height. He had been sitting on the bench and hence was completely out of sight. He did not say a word as he must have been awestruck by what he had just seen and since he was done with his clothes, just walked away without a second glance.

It really must have been terrible for him as I had acted like a banshee on fire. Meanwhile, I got up and began to collect my dry clothes and having done so walked with my basket to the elevator when I realized that I may not have been alone during that time of the day.

Just then, the elevator descended to the basement and when the doors opened, I was relieved to see that I was alone. To my embarrassment, my crotch had a wet patch which stood out prominently. I shut my eyes tightly and brought the basket of clothes to hide this from prying eyes.

I was sweating profusely when the elevator stopped on the ground floor and in stepped a short elderly man. He greeted me merrily and gave me a sweet smile while I responded to him trying to be as casual as possible. Just then the elevator came up to my floor and I literally ran out waving hurriedly at the smiling old man. I was panting feverishly as I shut the door behind me. I threw the basket of clothes on the floor and rushed to my bedroom where I collapsed on my bed, laughing in relief as well as the hilarity of the situation. I had not known that I was so close to becoming a nymphomaniac. I even came to think that I could have done what I did in the presence of others who could have been there in the Laundromat. Setting all these thoughts aside I got up to take a shower and get ready for my visit later during the day.

When I met my friend at the coffee shop near her place, I had half a mind for sharing the event that had occurred that morning, but at the last moment stopped myself from becoming a fool. Debra was a warm hearted, stylish woman. She was unlike others I had met and there was a distinct flavor of fineness which had her stand out from the others. I had met quite by accident at the hospital when I had gone to the locker room to get into my scrub.

I had found her sitting on the bench, one leg pulled up, wiping away some fluids from her pussy. As I entered, she looked up and smiled casually and carried on her with her task. As I changed into my work clothes, she came over and started a conversation. "I just broke my relationship with this guy and felt I owed him one since we had never had sex all throughout our three months together," she said. "So as a gesture, I let him fuck me right here, in this very room," she continued in a casual tone.

She asked if I got to see him as I walked into the room. I looked questioningly at her because the only person I had passed a little while ago was the director of the hospital Peter Horton. I made a mock face. And then in the matter of a few minutes, we became friends.

Debra was actually Dr. Debra Fleming, doing her last month of internship at the hospital. She had had a brief affair with the director towards the closing months of her internship. She had learnt from one of her predecessors that it was very important that he put in some good recommendations in her letter of satisfactory completion of the internship. Peter Horton had always had an eye for good looking women in his workplace and he loved to hold them captive, impressing them with his affluence and anecdotes of yesteryears.

In the middle of his conversations with the women who came under his spell, he would drop strong hints of sexual intent, most of which was brushed aside by the women in question. Debra, too, had to face this predicament one such day and she had felt embarrassed then. However she had come to terms of the situation when one day she had failed to report to work and her section of the ward was severely hit for want of experienced manpower. She had gone out of town, visiting an acquaintance and had missed the last train for the day. The following day the train services had been cancelled since there had been a storm.

Debra had managed to make it back to work on the third day and she had been summoned by the director only to be reprimanded with a suspension. If that was to happen, Debra's career was going to be in shambles. She had at that very moment made up her mind to give Peter Horton her best blow job ever. That way she could stay on his good side and yet not sleep with him for whatever he was worth.

From then on there was no turning back, as she would voluntarily go to his office late in the evening and just give him her lip service. The previous day she had been given her recommendation letter and the very next day Peter had just landed in the women's locker room unannounced.

It was almost 7:00 a.m. and there was no one around except Debra who had just finished her night shift. As she had stepped out of the showers, naked, wiping her body with her towel was when Peter had startled her with his presence. Watching her in the nude, her large breasts and hairless pussy had driven him crazy and he literally begged her to surrender to his whims. It was then Debra had allowed him to lick her pussy and suck at her nipples. Aroused, she had finally given him a fuck and just after, I had walked in. It was when she related to me her entire experience, did I feel that I could trust her with my own inner turmoil. That was when we had set a date to see each other that fateful Saturday.

I was keen to meet her and reached our meeting place just in time. She waved and I walked to the table. Debra looked pretty in her maroon outfit as it went well with her skin tone. Her breasts stood out prominently and anyone eyeing her would certainly get a hard on. We ordered burgers and Coke as I sat and listened to her animated talks.

She had been excited as she had just received a phone call from Dr. Jorgen's office. Dr Ivan Jorgen was the most sought after plastic surgeon and the fraternity grapevine had it that he was looking for a physician to be part of his medical team. She had applied with little or no hope and had been pleasantly surprised to receive a phone call from his office to meet him on Monday. This had triggered a knee jerk reaction from her and she had hurriedly called me to meet her and said that she had plans for us both to have "some girly fun." I had been intrigued the whole of the previous day and even taken pains to do my Brazilian wax so my pussy looked at its pink best. It was just a notion but I had gone ahead and done it and there I was in my shortest skirt without any bra or panties. This was the very first time I had attempted to do it but I felt good.

Debra had planned for us to meet her two male doctor friends at the café and I was now in the realm of excitement. The mere mention of the prospects had sent my pussy juices flowing. I tried to hide the sensation by crossing my legs once too often having her believe that I was being turned on. Just what she had in mind, I guess. Within a few moments we were joined by two handsome men who looked more like Hollywood stars than the doctors we were meant to meet.

Dave and Bob were both resident doctors at the hospital and I had overheard the nurses talking about them with blushes and wishful thoughts. Dave seemed to be quite an extrovert, whom I liked and he chose to sit by my side. His hands went straight to my waist and after the initial ice breaking, began to tell the group about the plan of the day. His uncle owned a villa just by the seaside and we were to go there and spend our weekend. Debra let out a loud " Yippeeee" which had some heads in the café turn to our directions. I did the same but in my mind. The flow of my pussy juice seemed like someone had left the taps open so I quickly excused myself to be let out for a visit to the washroom. While I was moving out, Dave's hand came over my buttocks, I bet he had at that moment learnt that I wasn't wearing panties.

I smiled and walked quickly to the washroom. Inside I tried to catch my breath as here was the moment I was waiting for. I had never been touched by any man, never mind felt or fucked. I did not have to worry about my hymen or blood because during my numerous uses of the vibrators, I had allowed the wench in me to live up to her expectations. And now it was going to be the real thing. I just could not wait for the experience. I took my time over relieving myself and then took some toilet paper to soak the juices around my cunt.

Wiping myself clean, I flushed and walked out to the sink. I took some more paper napkins and soaking them, dabbed my face. After a final look over, I walked out of the room and that is when I saw the look in the eyes of Dave. He was talking to the others but his eyes, mischievously were telling me that he knew what was I was up to. I blushed slightly as he got up from his seat and let me take mine. I settled in and just then our food and beverages arrived. I offered my plate to Dave and he took a cursory bite of my burger and a sip from my glass. He asked the waiter over and asked her to get him the same while Bob settled for some chicken salad.

As to when owe finished eating, I did not know. All I could recall was Bob picking up the tab and we all stepped out into the parking lot. There stood one of the most beautiful cars I had laid my eyes on. It was a red convertible. Dave and I got into the back seats while Bob and Debra got into the front and we whizzed through the city. The weather was a bit cloudy but it did show a lot of promise.

My skirt had already ridden up quite a bit and it caught Dave's eye. Within no time he had his right hand on my thigh and I felt the initial quiver run up my spine. He moved closer as we drove through the countryside. I could smell his cologne faintly but it was doing wonders for my senses. I was just smiling as Bob kept shouting over the sound of the engine and the wind. All I could gather was that we were going to have the times of our lives. I did not know how or when but I found my hand creeping on Dave's thighs as I rubbed it through the fabric of his slacks. I kissed his neck without being asked or told. I was doing all this for the very first time. Just then I felt his fingers stroking my pussy lips and I let out a moan. All this was happening out in the open for anyone to see. Even Debra stole a peek and looked quite pleasantly surprised.

The edge of Dave's hand seemed like a blunt knife cutting my cunt into two parts. Now I did not hesitate and went for his cock through his pants and I wasn't even surprised to find it hard and it felt beautiful to feel. I held it lovingly as it was the only thing that could make me and keep me happy. In my mind I was being lifted upwards, towards heaven as the eagerness between my legs grew more intense.

After about an hour's drive, we could smell the ocean. Just beyond the elevated road we saw the first sight of the surf. Now I did not even feel like hiding my erotic feelings and I was open to myself and to Dave.

"Promise me that you will do what you like with my body," I whispered into his ear.

Dave put his arm around my shoulder and looked me in the eye. "I promise I shall ravage your body to my heart's content," he said. I smiled and cuddled closer to him taking my other hand to run it on his hairy chest.

As soon as we arrived at the gorgeous villa I knew that Bob had been right. The structure overlooked the ocean front from practically all sides. It was a modern design with floor to ceiling glass windows and it had a sunken living room. I ran up the stairs and called out to Dave to hurry behind me. Dave was held up in talking to Bob over what to do next while Debra was already taking off her clothes to go skinny dipping in the water of the sea.

All I was interested in right then was Dave's cock deep inside my pussy and nothing more. I came upon this beautiful and elegant bedroom which was very well crafted. It had a low bed and the covers were silken to feel. I took off my dress by sliding it over my head. I opened up my hair and just flung myself on the bed.

"Dave," I called out and now the desperation in my voice was obvious.

He was in the doorway and he laid his eyes on me. I was lying on my back; legs bent at the knee and spread wide open. My breasts heaved as I was breathing quite heavily. My moist pussy glistened in the faint sunlight and my hands had clenched the bed sheet. Now my mind was in control as I even raised my waist above the surface and moved it up and down suggestively. Dave could not wait any longer either as he tore off his shirt and came over my body. He planted a delicious kiss on my lips. This drove me higher and I held his head tightly not wanting to let go. He withdrew his tongue after a while and brought his mouth to my neck, kissing it lightly and running his lips up and down the length of my neck.

Goosebumps appeared all over my body and a quaint tingling sensation made its presence felt in my body. He had rested his knees between my spread legs while he supported his upper body by placing his hand each next to my waist. He was only touching my neck with his neck and this was driving me crazy. Then he bit me on my neck; more of a nibble. I squirmed under him, wanting to be touched all over.

He knew exactly how to drive a woman crazy by her wants and he knew it well. I let my hands do the talking as I opened his belt and pants, pulling them down. Dave stood up and removed all his clothing and climbed over my body once again. This time he came over my body completely resting it over mine. His cock was snug between my legs and his face was buried between my breasts. Ahhhhhh!

it felt wonderful with his body over mine completely encompassing it with his weight and girth. He kissed my lips yet again before bringing his mouth over my breasts while I squirmed as I had never, never felt anything like this before and I wanted more of it. He sucked my nipple until it became painfully hard but I held his head almost lovingly and ran my hands over his hair.

He tried to take my whole breast in his mouth and his teeth bit into its softness. His grip on my back was firm as he moved his attention to the other breast and the tingling sensation made me hornier. He moved his tongue on my navel for a while and then he went straight to my pussy. Initially I felt that a live snake had entered my pussy that I even looked down. That was more than bliss and it felt so good. The way he tickled my clit made my body wriggle wildly and I gripped his hair with both my hands.

I resisted pulling his hair so I shifted my hands to fist the bed sheets. I was beginning to feel like a wild bronco as my body buckled and I was trying to be still at the same time. Dave stood up and wiped his mouth with a napkin from the bedside table. He then brought his erect and hard cock between my legs while I held it to guide it inside. I did not know what to expect as never before had any real cock entered that region. I raised my torso to meet the impact of his cock and felt it plunge in a single stroke. Ahhhhhhhhhh! I moaned loudly as I felt my pussy walls cover the hard member all over and as he started to stroke it in and out; I felt a wave of orgasm rising like tidal waters from the pit of my cunt. I almost felt the tingling in my ears and with my eyes shut, I felt I was moving amongst clouds.

One moment it felt tight around my middle and the next I was floating. Meanwhile Dave had felt his flood rising too and that's when he pulled out his cock spraying his semen all over my stomach. Dave fell over my body, exhausted by the whole episode. So that was what a fuck felt like? I thought. It was one of the most wonderful experiences I had ever had. I had nothing to worry about now since I knew I had Dave to fuck me as and when I wanted.

AUTHOR'S NOTE

Readers: I want to expand a few of the stories to see where the characters can be explored further. If there are any of the stories that you would like to read more about again, I'd love to hear from you!

Visit my blog at www.sterlingklemm.com

Join my newsletter for free exclusive previews
www.sterlingklemm.com/in

Follow me on Twitter at
www.twitter.com/sterlingklemm

Like my page on Facebook at
www.facebook.com/sterlingklemm1

Discover my books at major ebook retailers everywhere.